Final Stanzas

Also by Grant Tracey

Lovers & Strangers
Parallel Lines and the Hockey Universe
Playing Mac: A Novella in Two Acts
  and Other Scenes

Final Stanzas

Stories

Grant Tracey

Twelve Winters Press

Sherman, Illinois

Published by Twelve Winters Press.

P. O. Box 414 • Sherman, Illinois 62684-0414 • twelvewinters.com

Final Stanzas was first published by Twelve Winters Press in 2015.

Cover and interior page design by TWP Design.

Cover art copyright © 2015 Angela Wakefield. *Fifth Avenue*, Manhattan, New York. Visit www.ascotstudios/angela_wakefield. htm. Used by permission. All rights reserved.

Author photo copyright © 2015 Mitchell D. Strauss.

ISBN
978-0-9861597-1-8

Printed in the United States of America

Acknowledgments

The author thanks the following journals for publishing the stories in this collection: *Ascent* ("Turnstiles"); *Passages North* ("Seeing Red, Feeling Blue"); *Aethlon: the Journal of Sport Literature* ("Ossining, 1918"); *North Dakota Quarterly* ("Carl D'Amato"); *Cactus Heart* ("The Hermit Finds Solace"); *The Pedestal* ("Dead Flowers"); *South Dakota Review* ("Used and Abused"); *Fat City Review* ("Faraway Girl"); *Green Hills Literary Lantern* ("Written on the Sky"); and *Fiction Fix* ("According to Chelsea"). "Written on the Sky" was also nominated for a Pushcart Prize.

Contents

For Jeremy & Effy

Final Stanzas

You're all right, kid. I like guys who are honest with themselves. Stay that way.

—James Cagney, as Eddie Bartlett
in *The Roaring Twenties*

Turnstiles

❦

WHEN JOHNNY BETZ SAW JEANNIE BETZ HE wasn't sure it was really her. It had been quite a few weeks—outside of lengthy, odd phone calls—since they'd sat down and talked, and he felt like a secret agent, hiding behind pocket-book racks, staring at his assignment from inside a newsstand at the Bloor-Yonge subway exchange. She wore an orange wool coat and white boots that came up to her knees. Her hair flipped back from her forehead in a sassy wave that he hadn't seen before. It was clipped and cut above the collar. She appeared pensive, worrying her upper lip, waiting. Let her wait.

It all started two years ago with the war and Johnny's graduation from Macalester four months after the Tet Offensive. Suddenly his deferment was up, and he had very conflicted feelings about killing people who had never done him any harm. He didn't believe in the domino theory and saw American forces in Vietnam as unwanted intruders in a distant land, Prosperos to their Calibans. Later that summer, Janis Joplin scrawled an autograph across Johnny's draft card and wrote: "please, don't go." Two weeks after Janis's Detroit concert and much anguish followed by late-night conversations with his father, a veteran of the Korean conflict, Johnny left Ypsilanti, Michigan. With the help of underground connections he found work in Toronto and eventually met Jeannie.

Jeannie lived in the apartment next door and was often up late, listening gently to Leonard Cohen records. One eventful night, steam flooded the halls like swatches of fog. She had been trying to warm her apartment and wasn't about to ask for help (she managed a boutique on Yonge Street after all and was freethinking, a feminist, and hip on fashion—Coco Chanel's hats a favorite accessory), so she kept wheeling the radiator dial, until it wedged and wisps of heat shimmered and she lost sight of her hands. "You need to wear a towel," he said, upon entering the apartment. "This room is a sauna." She laughed, handed him a hot-pan holder, and watched, coughing, as he spun the stuck knob, cranking it back to its rightful place. "I'm really not this klutzy," she insisted, and then offered him a Fresca.

Over the next few months, mainly Tuesday and Saturday nights, they stopped in the halls or in each other's apartment to talk about music: she liked Cohen, Joni Mitchell, and Creedence; he admired Bob Dylan, Jimi Hendrix, and Janis, of course. Jeannie was the youngest in a family of five. Her parents, the Mladans, immigrants from Macedonia, ran a corner variety store and lived with her big brother Stoyan in the apartment above it. Johnny didn't tell her much about his past, except he was an only child: his mom worked at a kitchen in the public schools; his dad sold furnaces and although disappointed in the outcome of Johnny's exile surprisingly supported his son and in general the withdrawal of forces from Vietnam.

Jeannie found Johnny to be so brave. It is easy to do what your government tells you to do; it is much harder to not listen when they are wrong. But Johnny still felt conflicted—as if he had let down the two generations of Betzes before him who had served in Korea and the Great War. As he spoke of his feelings, she often smiled, leaned forward, right hand on left elbow, listening, nodding, soaking in his loss, his need to recover an irretrievable past. Six months after what they affectionately referred to as the "steam heat incident" they were married. Fourteen months after that, they separated.

At first, married life made Johnny happy. Periodically, she'd sneak up behind him, tickle his sides, shout "you're it," and let him chase her around the apartment, before the makeshift game of tag ended in an embrace and occasional lovemaking on the couch or the floor of the kitchen. Jeannie had the darkest eyes Johnny had seen—muddy charcoal—nearly as dark as her black hair, which wasn't silky smooth like the girls he knew in high school. Hers was heavy, thick, and a little coarse and belied the gentleness of her soul.

Jeannie also liked to hide his favorite coffee mug (white with a blue maple leaf)—in the freezer, on the scale in the bathroom, next to the scarves in the closet. He always found it and chuckled when he removed the crumpled note scrunched up inside: "I love you to the nth power." Sometimes he got even by flushing the toilet while she was showering. On the days that she didn't hide his coffee mug, Johnny felt a slight emptiness, as if some necessary ingredient were missing from his daily routine.

Eventually those occasional pangs of ennui spread into frequent occurrences, aches of dislocation—Canada wasn't America—and Johnny distanced himself, reading in the evenings instead of talking, and no longer leaving his own notes—"mywomanmywomanmywoman"—under her pillow, like he used to.

"There you are," she said, looking at her watch. A slender bracelet on her left hand glinted in the dusky light of the terminal. Under her right arm was a brightly wrapped package the size of a block of ice.

"Here I am." He shoved hands in pockets. The terminal was crowded and along a near wall, by the exit turnstiles, a musician with a rickety violin case played a guitar that couldn't possibly fit in the case. He sang "Wrote a Song for Everyone" in plaintive tones, loons on a lake.

Johnny didn't really care much for the back-to-basics rock of CCR—he liked edgier sounds, wah-wah pedals and feedback, anger and distortion.

"What about 'Fortunate Son'?" Jeannie said. "That was pretty edgy." She dropped a quarter in the violin case. "Thanks for coming."

For a second Johnny wasn't quite sure if she was talking to him or the guitarist. Johnny wiped his chin and quietly sighed. "When are we going to tell them?"

"Soon. It would kill them to know."

"No, it wouldn't."

Yes, it would, she pleaded. Her parents were from the old world and divorce wasn't something that happened in the old world.

"Divorce? We're just separated."

"Well—that too didn't happen. Maybe for a night, but not three weeks."

"Four—tomorrow. Tomorrow it's four."

"Well, anyway—" She gestured with her left hand, the thin bracelet catching on the fleshy underside of her palm. Nobody she or her family knew got separated. Aunt Ellen hated Uncle Mito, but they were still together.

"That's a ringing endorsement for marriage," Johnny said, as the guitarist changed keys for the final verse.

Jeannie had to admit that Johnny had a point, but she couldn't let her parents down, especially since they had been opposed to them getting married so young. She was only twenty then, and they worried that Johnny was all wrong for her. He was twenty-two, American and English-white; she was a Canadian and Macedonian with a touch of gypsy.

"Roma," Johnny corrected. "The preferred term is Roma."

"Roma," she said, annoyed. And more to the point, her parents and older brothers (Mito in his mid-forties and Stoyan, thirty-eight) always treated her like a little kid, the baby of the family. "God, I hate being the baby and I don't want them preaching to me."

"Well, you are the baby. I mean technically speaking."

"Thanks."

The exit turnstiles stuttered. Johnny bruised his thigh and had to push the wheel of X's with his hip to get it to click over. Jeannie, of course, had no problems. The turnstile was like her life, turning terrifically for her.

What had she to overcome? Her parents sheltered her. They all loved each other. Her father never spoke a cross word to Jeannie's mother. There were no drinking problems, no late night fights and broken dishes, no infidelities or a dark bowling ball heaved through a television set—none of that—and "that" wasn't something Johnny wanted to think about now, not really, but it was part of where he came from. By contrast, Jeannie's temperament—except when she was talking to her family—was so low key—she rarely dwelled on sad things.

Outside, brisk autumn air forced Johnny to tuck his chin into the folds of his jacket collar. The sky was heavy with rain. Johnny wanted to remind Jeannie that Stoyan wasn't that sold on him either and probably thought he too was a baby. Jeannie's older brother often walked around the living room with a fishing hat pushed back on his head, a rum-and-Coke in one hand, and a golf putter in the other, saying she was crazy. "You can't marry the first guy you sleep with," he had said one night when he thought Johnny wasn't listening, lost in the adjacent kitchen, searching for a beer.

Johnny also sensed a thinly veiled anti-American sentiment whenever he was in the presence of Stoyan. Night after night as clips from the conflict in Vietnam were shown on the evening news, Stoyan's voice would fill the spaces of Dedo's living room as he shouted to Johnny. "I mean, I like the people. Nicest people in the world—Americans. But your government is fucking crazy." "I can't disagree with you," Johnny often acknowledged, hoping that the hockey game would soon start.

Hockey. He played it in Michigan as a kid, and he

loved Canadians' passion for the sport—its mix of football-like violence with the athletic grace of ballet. Hockey took him outside of all this—the war, the past, his problems with love. Hell, he wished there was a game now that he could retreat into, the snick-snick of skates was a soothing sound, instead of the silences between them and this charade they were about to play for her parents. "You need to tell them."

"I will." She stopped to adjust the purse strap sliding off her shoulder. Her right hand rested on her hip. "But not yet. It's Dedo's birthday." He was turning seventy. Jeannie checked her face in a small compact. "I appreciate you agreeing to all this. I mean—you know—going through this."

"What did we get him?"

"A blanket." She adjusted the bulky block of a package against her hip. "Afghan."

Johnny nodded and fought an urge to place his hand through her arm and walk along Yonge Street, as if they were a happy couple. But he was living in a separate apartment and she was interested in a colleague at work. At least he thought she was. He wasn't sure, but she sure talked about the guy a lot. He wrote poems or something, had published a few, and was regarded by one editor as the next Raymond Souster, whoever the fuck he is. Johnny majored in English, published a story in Macalester's student-run literary journal, but he was no poet—just a clerk, now, on the seventh floor of an office.

The sky was an asphalt umbrella. Lightning jagged the dark. "I like what you did to your hair," he lied, still unsure of what to do with his hands.

THE APARTMENT SMELLED OF OKRA BEEF STEW, ZILNIC and a thick heavy coffee that had traces of chocolate in it. Johnny loved the mix of old-world cuisine with new-world vitality. And this family was vital. Stoyan hustled about, mixing drinks, spinning a putter in his left hand, while handing out party favors, and offering rum-and-Cokes. Johnny never wanted one but that never stopped Stoyan from asking. Dedo Nick, Jeannie's father, in his old-man slippers with fuzzy fringes, smiled now and then and spoke only in a gravel of Macedonian. Sophia, his wife, helped distribute snack plates of dark olives and feta cheese. Neither Ellen nor Mito was there. Ellen, a skip on a local curling team, had a match that night, and Mito was just too busy to get away from the office. He was a graphic designer, independent, Jeannie said, and Mito's office was in his home. "So you telling me, he can't get away," she mumbled.

Johnny nodded, his party hat slipping to the left, the itchy string irritating his neck.

Babo Sophie tapped Johnny's hand, said he looked good, and offered him olives and feta.

He smiled, finding it difficult to follow her words, but he concentrated on her face and sensed her favor towards him. He was family now. Sort of, he guessed.

The Mladans talked about cousins, especially thirty-something Virginia who was serious about a guy who still collected hockey cards and lived in his parents' basement. They also talked about the old country, Canada, jobs, lack of jobs, and the new immigrants, Pakistanis especially and how they smelled funny. "Shit on

8

a stick," Stoyan said about them, as if he was never the child of immigrants, and then he turned his attention to the article in *Life Magazine* that showed pictures of all the American dead in Vietnam. "Did you see that?" he asked, as if Johnny were somehow accountable for the actions of the Pentagon.

"Yeah." He bit his lower lip. "Yeah, I did. That was like two years ago."

"Last year—the summer—all you hear on the news is about kill counts—so many Cong killed—but my God—"

"It's actually Viet Minh, not Viet Cong," Johnny corrected.

Stoyan shook his head. One of the fishing hooks in the blue band of his hat looked like it might fall out. "And what about the space program?—collecting rocks—shouldn't they put that money to better use like education?"

Babo Sophie sensed Johnny's discomfort and with a raised hand told Stoyan, "dosta, dosta," and then complimented Johnny for the beautiful bracelet his wife was wearing. She touched the thin silver. "Much money, yes?" she asked with her eyes.

Johnny shrugged.

Stoyan too touched the bracelet's outer edge, leaving half a thumb print against the jewelry's smooth sheen. "Not bad. How much that set you back?"

"I don't know."

"Wow. It's nice."

"Yeah." Johnny nodded and Jeannie smiled in his direction before making an awkward face, and then pushed away from the table and asked Babo if she needed any help getting supper ready. Seconds later, the lights in the apartment flashed. We were in for a bad storm, Stoyan said. According to the radio, anyway, there were power outages north in Barrie and Bradford. Jeannie shrugged and reached for a row of plastic cups. Johnny wondered where Jeannie got the bracelet. From the guy at work? The poetry guy? Maybe she just bought it for herself.

"You know what gets me about Americans?" Stoyan swung the putter above his shoe tops. "They have no idea about Canada. They come up here this time of year and they've got ski racks on their cars. I mean, it's October."

"No they don't," Jeannie said, a tower of china plates in her left hand, pressing against her thigh.

"They do. I swear. We get less snow than Buffalo for Chrissakes."

Rain pounded the rooftop and ran down the narrow windows of the apartment. Streetlights across the way looked like they belonged in a French painting.

"Johnny, how many provinces does this country have?" Stoyan challenged.

"Ten."

"Very good. Most Americans don't even know who our Prime Minister is."

"Johnny's not American, anymore," Jeannie said.

"Pierre Elliott Trudeau, Prime Minister." Johnny paused, looking at his fingers and thinking about Jeannie's bracelet. "And, well, as far as provinces go, ten, unless you count Minnesota as the eleventh."

Jeannie laughed, wrinkles forming at the corner of her eyes. Stoyan didn't seem to get the joke. Johnny explained—Americans often refer to Canada as the 51st state or even worse, America's hat, but from a Canadian perspective Minnesota's the eleventh province. "We don't want any other states. Just Minnesota. Hockey country. And maybe the Upper Peninsula of Michigan."

"Now that's funny." Stoyan laughed, tapping his putter against the edge of the Formica table. "Jeannie, where did you get those boots? They sure look like they're made for walking." He laughed again.

AS THE MLADANS ATE THE BIG BIRTHDAY DINNER, their voices rising and rising, they were like guitarists in a rock-and-roll band, turning up for solos and forgetting to turn back down. Whenever Jeannie spoke to one of them on the phone, her voice would surge until in the end she was yelling. "I'm not yelling," she'd say, punching Johnny in the shoulder. "I'm just discussing." "You're yelling now, as you *discuss* things with me. Bring it back down," he'd say while tickling her sides. "That's how we talk. I'm ethnic." And then he'd kiss her, but he could never match her volume so they rarely argued.

Listening now to the crashing waves of reedy voices, the mix of dialects, Johnny enjoyed his space from the outside. Many of their stories focused on Dedo and his inability to understand English. "'Make your par?' he'd ask customers in the store instead of 'Beg your pardon?' 'Make your par?' Hilarious," Stoyan said.

Johnny smiled faintly for he was falling away, drifting from the moment playing out in front of him. It was a feeling he had since leaving the US, a kind of absurdist despair, a lingering pain, no beginning, no end, as if he were Albert Camus's Sisyphus, pushing a rock up a hill and having to push it again and again and again.

Why couldn't he just will those dark feelings away and be happy with Jeannie? Why did he feel as if he were living and moving in a driftless area, like astronauts floating weightless in space? Because those rocks, the emotional joys of life, could never stay at the top of the hill, but the journey was worth it, the impermanence of the journey was worth it, wasn't it, all that pushing, because Jeannie was just so gentle and real.

It was *his* fault that he and Jeannie were separated. Somehow during the course of their relationship, he had got it into his head that she had fallen into the idea of loving him and didn't love him for who he really was: the guy who could get grumpy when his feet got wet in the rain; the guy who hated to get picked last at the company softball game; the guy who wanted to scream down all of the digs and sideways comments tossed his way from his brother-in-law to the people at work to the media who wrote about "draft dodgers." He had feared that his was but a political marriage.

Moreover, when they made love it wasn't passionate. Jeannie was withdrawn, sometimes gasping briefly for air because intimacy scared her a little. Other times she'd lie there gently while he came, and then patted his back. She always seemed grateful, full of affection and admiration, but he wanted that elusive emotional commitment that the poets—probably the guy at the boutique—wrote about.

Anyway, as the weeks stretched by, and as he watched her now, smiling, moving between her parents and big brother, navigating a space for Johnny and herself within the slightly murky waters of their anti-American sentiment (they were talking about Nam again), he experienced a deep longing, like he felt at the subway terminal when he had wanted to put his hand through the triangle of space of her flexed elbow, or when he got stuck in the stuttering wheel of the turnstile and briefly feared that he wouldn't be able to follow her out the exit. Damn it, he wanted to kiss her, to have bought her that goddamn bracelet. As they ate supper and side plates of cheese zilnick (Dedo's favorite), Johnny realized his mistake.

He hadn't loved *her* enough. It wasn't that she didn't love him—she always had. Her love for him wasn't idealized—she didn't just admire his politics and want to help him become Canadian, keep him safe. No, they loved the same books: Saul Bellow and Margaret Laurence. Believed in unions and higher education and voted NDP. Cared about the environment and used reusable cloth bags when they shopped for groceries so as to save on paper. They also cared about the rights of women and thought "free love" was but a male construct to exploit the fairer sex. No, the ennui, the inability to trust in love, was his problem. He left his country, his family, and now he was leaving her and the family he created in Canada. He couldn't stay connected to people.

How often had he contacted his mother and father since coming to Canada? When Jeannie suggested he call his folks, he'd rather read or go outside on the balcony and smoke a cigar. When she suggested they take ballroom dancing to help bring them closer, he laughed, and said, "I don't dance." When she suggested that he make a Monday or Wednesday meal like he used to, he opted for frozen dinners. He was retreating from their life. But tonight he was with her again, the four weeks apart was too long a gap, and as she smiled at her parents and looked great in a brown cashmere sweater that highlighted the supple curves of her small breasts, he wanted to tell her all of this. Tonight, he felt that maybe the charade of the happy couple, the performance they were playing was or could be real. They could do this, he wanted to do this, to be with her, to try and become a better lover, to believe in love, and being loved.

Dedo had two more helpings of zilnick and Jeannie told him to be careful, to not eat too much—it had a lot of butter in it, take it easy.

"Take what easy," Stoyan said. "It's his birthday. And you could afford to eat a little more." He pointed his fishing hat at Jeannie. "You look skinny. Lost five-ten pounds, maybe?"

"She looks great," Johnny corrected.

"You haven't even touched your okra stew."

"I'm a vegetarian," she said.

"Since when?"

"Six months now."

"Well, can't you just pick out the beef?" He was standing away from the table.

"Stoyan, the taste has spread to everything—the fat. You can't just pick out the beef."

"Well that's stupid. You need meat," he said.

"No, you don't." She had been eating rice and beans, like people in the Third World, and doing just fine. Her energy was up; she never felt more vital. She was discovering the joys of whole grains, too. "Dad still doesn't sell Wonder Bread in the store because he knows that enriched stuff's no good for you. He just never figured out the truth about meat. It's bad for your heart."

"Meat is protein. We're wired to eat meat."

"I like veggies, and I'm discovering a variety of ways of cooking with tofu."

"Toe what? Are you insane?" Jeannie's new diet was a strange challenge of some kind that just didn't make much sense to Stoyan. His fishing hat was clenched hard in his left hand and instead of talk-yelling, like was the Mladans' wont, he was screaming.

"I don't think you should talk to her that way," Johnny said. "She's not stupid. She's not insane. She's—" His lower lip was quavering but he wasn't about to back down. "She's entitled to her opinions—"

"What are you going to do? Bomb me and my beliefs back to the stone age, General Westmoreland?"

"He's not an American anymore," Jeannie shouted at Stoyan. "He's a Canadian. After he married me, he got his citizenship."

Now Johnny too stood away from the table and looked over at Jeannie and sighed. The chair vibrated under him and a slight rattle filled the silence and twitched up his left arm before stopping at his elbow. Her response, although supportive, wasn't quite right. Yes, he was a Canadian, but he was also an American. And he wasn't embarrassed about being one.

"I'm sorry," she said, realizing her mistake.

"She's a free person." He shrugged, removed his party hat, and sulked toward the apartment's living room.

From there he could still hear the conversation's fall-out—they were loud. He picked up a putter leaning against a radiator and tapped three or four golf balls resting against the legs of the vinyl-covered couch.

"What makes you feel so superior, huh?" Jeannie asked. Canadians were supposed to be humble—this was such bullshit. A Formica chair scraped against the floor. She too was about to leave. Babo said stay, it was Dedo's birthday, but Jeannie said, "I'm sorry, Ma, but Stoyan just can't treat my husband this way."

And then they started speaking in Macedonian, perhaps to keep Johnny out of the loop on their private conversation, but more likely to help Dedo and Babo enter into the flow of dialogue. Babo's voice was full of tears.

Johnny couldn't understand Dedo's words exactly, but listening to the crunch of his gravelly voice was like witnessing Hendrix playing "The Star-Spangled Banner," his guitar converting absent words into emotional truths. Dedo felt Stoyan was wrong and it appeared that he was defending Jeannie's husband.

Stoyan's words shrugged after that. They were no longer on full volume, and he apologized again to Jeannie, to his mother and father, and admitted that he'd always been jealous of Americans. He spoke now in English, as if, perhaps, he wanted Johnny to hear his explanation, to apologize indirectly instead of face-to-face. Americans were so confident, Stoyan said, sitting down. They always were, and yesterday he had lost out on a promotion for chief engineer with de Havilland Aircraft. He had been there for twenty years, twenty, count them, twenty, doing a fine job in their designs department, but he hadn't moved up as fast as that young thirty-something from Princeton. "So, he gets the pay raise." He sighed. "Eat what you like. But vegetarianism? I mean honestly." Silverware touched plates, glasses tapped Formica.

"Hey, when are we going to watch the hockey game?" Johnny shouted.

"Turn it on," Stoyan said. "We'll be right there."

BEFORE RETIRING TO THE LIVING ROOM TO WATCH the game, Dedo opened his gifts: Jeannie's orange and brown Afghan to stay warm during damp nights of TV viewing and a gold watch that glowed in the dark and would help him find his way to the bathroom at 4 a.m., Stoyan joked.

By the time they turned on the solid-state, color television, it was already 2-1 for Buffalo, but Jacques Plante had made several key saves, keeping the Leafs in the game. Sabres goalie Roger Crozier was hot that night too, stopping the Leafs' Davey Keon on a break-away. During intermission, Dedo shook his head and mumbled something about why don't they show more Blackhawks games—GM Tommy Ivan was from the old country.

"Ivan—that doesn't sound Macedonian," Johnny said.

"He changed his name. His parents are from like the same village as Dedo," Jeannie said. Ivan was born in To-ronto.

"Really?"

Dedo also liked Johnny Weissmuller, the Tarzan guy, Jeannie translated, and Boris Karloff. Weissmuller was from somewhere in Romania and Karloff was from near Zhelevo.

"Karloff's English," Johnny whispered to Jeannie and she squeezed his hand so he didn't say anything too loudly.

In the second period the Leafs tied the game before Buffalo tough guy Reg Fleming fired a low slap-shot between the post and Plante's skate to once again give Buffalo the lead. Twice during the period the lights in the apartment flickered and the TV screen turned to buzzing bees. Somewhere in the middle of the period, during a boring spell of neutral-zone hockey, Jeannie once again squeezed Johnny's hand before getting sodas for everyone.

"I don't think you guys should try to get home to-night," Stoyan said from the radiator. The putter resembled a marching baton in his right hand. "The couch opens up. It's comfortable. Hell, it's late. And it's raining like crazy."

Johnny looked over at Jeannie whose face was an open expression he couldn't read. The eyebrows were steady, still, the lips parted. It was as if he could map on her face whatever feelings, meanings he wanted to.

"We could play a round of golf in the morning—if the greens aren't under a lake," Stoyan said.

"I'm terrible at golf."

"Good. I'm not. I'll kick your ass." And then he laughed. He often found his own jokes amusing.

"I—we—can stay." Jeannie absently caressed the bracelet with the sleeve of her sweater. "We can stay," she repeated.

Johnny nodded. Rain beat out a rhythm of an angry tap dancer. He wasn't sure how this was all going to end. In a narrative poem, "Turnstiles," yet to be written by the kind of guy who perhaps gives a coworker an expensive bracelet, the estranged couple would play at being married, pretend to be dutiful and supportive of each other, make light jokes, eat and smile and watch the game. Then afterward, commit to polite conversation on the way to the bus stop. The final stanzas would capture a mood of loss and loneliness. Once inside the tunnel, "swatches of clothes, dark hats / her ribbon of bracelet, cars silver / little boxes heading / nowhere," they'd get stuck in the turnstiles—and he'd enjoy the captured seconds of immobility—she, gripping her bag, tight, against her shoulder would ready to take the Yonge Southbound to King; he regrettably would be heading for the Bloor East to Page. Just before leaving on separate trains, they'd part, and in a moment of elevated language, the poet's final stanza, the speaker would tell us that "they smiled, promising / to talk, tonight, tomorrow / but as doors hushed open / gaps, minded, they knew of / no new beginning / but the line's end." That wasn't the poem that Johnny would write. He wasn't sure what was in front of them, but it wasn't that. He sure hoped it wasn't. Besides, they weren't going anywhere tonight. He still had tonight.

And just then the Leafs' Paul Henderson flipped a backhand pass to number-nine Normie Ullman, who took it on his forehand and wristed it through Crozier's blocker side. A red light flashed, Babo and Jeannie and Johnny cheered, and as the goaltender sank to the ice, his right catch glove caught the crossbar, holding his slinky legs up, keeping him from falling any farther.

Seeing Red, Feeling Blue

❧

A S MIDNIGHT RUNS GO THIS WAS A PIP. IN COLLEGE, Dawn Shattuck often sought adventure at a moment's notice: a 2 a.m. run to get morning donuts from a mom-and-pop store in back of a Main Street pharmacy; a 3:30 in the morning cookout with two female friends who suddenly had a yen for grilled bratwurst on the quad. The university police weren't amused but the girls weren't breaking any laws. They were asked to "keep the smell down." Go figure. And just last semester, her final before the publication of her debut and critically acclaimed novel, *Seeing Red, Feeling Blue*, about an angry young twenty-something who sleeps with her mother's lover, Dawn raided several drugstores for Magnum condoms in order to make a balloon puppet of a professor *cum-laude* dictator— think Mussolini with a very small erection (needless to say, this condom was not a Magnum). Her gift, which hung in prophylactic effigy from his second-floor office window, wasn't discovered until mid-afternoon the next day. Even Dawn's Mom Deanna was mildly amused. She found the tiny attributes of the off-brand condom appropriate. "All that abuse of power—he must be compensating for a lack of something," she said one cold afternoon as they left a Chinese restaurant. Mom placed quote marks around the last word, then smiled, and tossed a white scarf over her left shoulder and further adjusted the racing glove on her stick-shift hand. She owned a vintage Datsun 240z and fancied herself something of a skillful adventurer, a Richard Petty of Toronto's Don Valley Parkway.

Much to Dawn's chagrin, however, Mom never did quite get jokes. Placing quote marks around "something" was an odd choice—it really wasn't indicative of clever wordplay on her part or even worthy of a chortle or sharp guffaw. Thus, she hadn't truly earned the gloves of diacritics she granted the word. Now if instead of quote marks around "something" she had placed them around say a word like "extensions" (his refusal to give one for a paper due and inability to get one for a female in the bedroom), well, then, that would be funny, a regular riot, Norton. (Dawn loved the stark minimalism of *The Honeymooners*).

Now, at 1:15 in the morning, Mom still wearing the gloves and Dawn sporting a faded red Dairy Queen T-shirt (inside sexual orientation joke) were hovering in the apartment of Mom's lover, Jonah Leland, possibly soon-to-be ex, and gobbling up all Mom's possessions, shoving them into threadbare blue nylon bags. "It's my stuff after all," she said, as way of apology, while biting her upper lip and cramming more and more DVDs, books, art supplies, and clothes into each bag. The wrinkles around Mom's eyes were slightly raised and her face look tired. So far ten blocky bags were lumped together and sagging with eclectic stuff. The plan was to haul it to Dawn's one-bedroom apartment and let it sit for a few days until things settled out with Jonah. Dawn feared that the "settling" process might stretch into a few months because Mom, who once ran a consignment shop and wore Mod clothes, was now currently unemployed.

"Take some of his shit, too. What the fuck." Dawn shrugged, scrunching a not-so-funny book on Canadian humor into an open space at the top of a bag.

"You think?"

"Why not?" She also insisted on kyping Jonah's thin pair of drumsticks with fine plastic tips. Her possibly soon-to-be ex (that's how Deanna referred to him, now, eschewing first and last names) was a jazz aficionado and in the late '50s, in one of Montreal's smoky bistros, had sat in on a set with Billie Holiday. He was just seventeen at the time, she nearing the end of her run, but the bourbon-smoked voice still held a gritty poignancy and during a set break, she leaned near his kit and between splashes of Jack Daniels toyed with his sticks, tapping them along her upper thighs.

"Why not?" Mom echoed Dawn and slid the drumsticks into another tight nylon corner. A Beta tape pushed through the fabric like an angry brick.

"Beta, Mom? Who watches Beta tapes? I don't even know why you want half this junk."

"They're rare Bergman films."

"Okay," Dawn conceded. She herself liked the edgy irony of Agnes Varda and if all she had of her work was on Beta then she'd keep them too. "Here. Take the Stan Getz records." Jonah loved Getz. Seven of the records slithered into another lopsided bag. Dawn also tossed in a small floor lamp shaped like a breast (44DD probably—the bags could stretch), a set of china plates (not made in China but Sherrill, New York), and the TV's remote control (the last the most brazen of all transgressions).

"Now, wait a minute, Hon, I don't want to be vindictive."

"Why not—he's a fucking jerk," Dawn said.

"Is he?" Mom's voice shaded into a challenge that Dawn hadn't felt since she graduated from junior high and said she wanted to learn Spanish so that she could work for the CIA. This was another one of Dawn's drifting jokes, full of ennui, but Mom thought she was serious and worried about her getting killed by a KGB agent as soon as she stepped off a plane in Panama or Nicaragua or some other such place. "I mean, really? I—let's not lay it all at his feet, huh?"

"Okay." Dawn had been playing the moment irreverently, but Mom's pensive mood contoured everything with complexity and ambiguity. "After all he had the affair," Dawn said, reminding Mom of why they were here. Business trips to Montreal. Textiles. Maria's tits.

"Don't be crude." Yes, Jonah Leland was fooling around with Maria Sauvage—a working girl of all things, Mom said, as if she had forever sloughed off her working class past. But that wasn't the real problem; it was much more complicated than that. Mom frowned and shrugged sadly. So, in the in-between time, while her possibly soon-to-be ex was out of town, Mom's midnight raid was an attempt to salvage her autonomy. Retreat with her possessions, then talk to Jonah when he returns on Tuesday and see where things stand. If she never took her stuff from the apartment she would never be able to establish her rights.

"I hope to put a scare in him," Mom said.

Scare? So Mom and the possibly soon-to-be ex were about to get back together? At least if Mom had her way they would.

Dawn smiled. She could understand Mom's need to haul her stuff away, but the blue bags of junk just had to go: Beta tapes? Okay save the Bergman, but the rest recorded at EP off of pre-digital cable? Please; clothes that looked like they belonged in Goodwill's refuse pile? Books that had been stored in a damp basement and had traces of green lines and rust-stained mildew spots? This stuff made the 1930s Dust Bowl look attractive. But Deanna was unlike Dawn. Sure Mom could rush along at 140 klicks on the Don Valley and beat anyone off the line zero to sixty, but she bottled things, like a regular Coca-Cola plant. She wasn't a writer like Dawn—converting life into art—she couldn't find leverage with words—she needed to act.

"I can't take the clicker." She handed it back to Dawn.

"All right. I'm glad you draw the line somewhere."

"Was that a joke?"

Dawn rolled her eyes with as much of a clichéd pout as she could muster, and then dropped the remote in her own bag, next to the Polaroid photographs she had found in a lower desk drawer. Three of the Polaroids featured Dawn naked from the chest up, an ill-advised night three years ago when Jonah asked her over while

Deanna was away at the Toronto Film Festival. The images were washed out, the light a dark orange. Dawn wore a maroon skirt and hard plastic hair clips. They matched the skirt. Accessories—she learned that from Mom (a holdover from her boutique days).

Mom pushed photographs of herself and the possibly soon-to-be ex by a tennis net into a ninth bag, and then looked around the room, her eyes wet glass. "We had a lot of good times."

Dawn trapped a laugh against her upper lip but couldn't hold it. It came out like chips of granite.

"We did have good times." The two of them had traveled to Russia and Ireland together. "He just doesn't want to touch me anymore." Everything was fine until she took classes at York University toward a BA in English. She was getting too smart for him.

Dawn nodded absently but didn't bother to remind her mother that of all the papers she had written, Dawn edited, proofed, and substantially revised most all of them. Mom's grades on her first efforts were C's and C-'s, the papers largely plot summaries or unsubstantiated appreciations of artistic genius, but there were no arguments. Dawn gave the papers theses, shaped the paragraphs so they contained point-first or point-last constructions, and helped Mom get nothing lower than an A- in the future.

If Jonah wanted to be mad at anyone it should have been Dawn, not Deanna. After all it was Dawn's brain on display, not her mother's, and yet she didn't hate Jonah, even though she pretended to, and he didn't hate her mental prowess. He loved her novel, said it was "like a mouthful of glass shards" (the ultimate compliment for a writer of witty emo-ennui). Three times he read it. "Five," Mom later confessed.

"You sure we can get this all in your snazzy car?" It had little space in the back and less in the trunk. "Isn't it like a Formula One model, registered with Indy or something?"

"Oh, get out." Mom laughed.

And with that they clomped down the stairs several times from the master bedroom. On each descent, Dawn pocketed one more item of Jonah's: a pair of red head bands, a tennis racket signed by Björn Borg, and a pair of ten-pound dumbbells. It was hard navigating the stairs with all this junk, but she managed.

THREE YEARS AGO, DAWN STRUGGLED WITH HER SEXUAL orientation. She wasn't out yet, but she didn't feel that she was "in" either. She liked who she liked—boys, girls— and bisexual seemed too narrow a term as did lesbian. Queer was better, because there was something in the word that was both perverse and edgy—abstractions that fit her nearly everyday mood of angst at social injustices everywhere.

And it was when she was in this state of identity flux and Mom away at a three-day film festival in Toronto that Jonah called her, saying that his dog was terribly sick and he felt lousy. King (a female dog—Jonah too had an impish sense of humor) was an Alaskan husky with two very different eyes—one blue, the other gray. She had an inoperable lump on her chest and Jonah was in tears calling King "Lumpy Rutherford" because he couldn't deal with the cancer (the dog eventually died six months later). Anyway, while he was calling King "old Lumpy," he asked Dawn to come over, watch a movie—he had just purchased a new TV—and we'll drink wine, even though she was underage and he knew that she was. *Caveat Emptor.*

"That's not quite the right phrase," she said. "Let the buyer beware?"

"Exactly." His tone hinted at something perhaps dangerous and on the margins of good taste.

So, even though she knew that his intentions weren't entirely fatherly or decent, forty minutes later they were standing in his living room, looking at an art piece that took up the far wall. It was white, with maybe a figure shielding his or her eyes from the sun in the lower left corner. "What the fuck is it?" she said.

"To the point. Always. I like that. 'What the fuck is it?' Pithy. Nice. It looks like a bunch of snow to me. Okay, maybe a schmuck on a mountainside during a snowstorm. See him on the—"

"—lower left?"

"Yeah. That's it."

Deanna had bought it—on her own—from an expensive art gallery near Bloor and Spadina, next to the museum. A thousand-dollar-piece of shit.

"I like it," Dawn said.

"Figures." He rubbed the edge of his jaw and smiled. His face had a softness to it, as if as he got older he became more feminine, the masculine lines in the cheeks and eyes becoming more milky, smooth. His hair, tight curled and gray, was distinguished like a Roman emper-

or or someone who loved issuing parking tickets, but his eyes were warm, friendly, and like his dog, each one was different. The pupil of his left was twice the size of the right and a little darker. "You Shattuck girls stick together, huh?"

Dawn smiled. Was that true? During her final year of high school, Dawn fought her mother constantly because she was a poser with her high-fashion Go-go boots and scarves wound carelessly around her neck and flipped over a shoulder. Whenever Mom got into conversations, Dawn cringed. Mom was full of platitudes, making nice. Besides the tossed off, all purpose "oh, get out," to make light of any situation, there was the crazy cosmic defense for the random chaos of the universe. It went something like this: Mom nodding at the bad news, tilting her head left, tapping her upper lip three times, and quietly intoning, "It must be the ions in the air." Ions! Mom, that says nothing. Ions! Once when Mom mistakenly said, "It must be the enzymes in the air," Dawn cut her off in front of her guest and shouted, "Enzymes are in your mouth, Ma. Not the air. Unless God is constantly spitting at us!"

Anyway, Mom's white painting had nineteen or twenty little spots of red in the upper right corner, splashes of neon rain. Dawn tried to make sense of the contrast of colors while playing with King's ears, sipping wine, and slipping into a buzzed haze. In the interim, between red and white, Jonah pointed out the finer details of each chart they were listening to, from the drummer's cross-sticking to the saxophonist's transpositions of the root fifth, and the trumpeter's improvisational tangents.

Dawn didn't understand much of what he was saying—she was a fan of '70s punk rock—but his enthusiasm for jazz was infectious.

They sipped more wine and talked about textiles (something or other to do with plain, satin, or twill weaves) and then he asked about the project she was working on for her school newspaper. She was the managing editor.

In 1950, York University planted a time capsule somewhere behind the then-new journalism building. The capsule (according to articles written back then) was full of offbeat personal items (Bee Hive hockey photos and big band records), essays on "The World of Tomorrow" written by the class of '51, and an early draft of Morley Callaghan's *The Loved and the Lost* which would eventually win Canada's Governor General Award for fiction. All of this and much more was allegedly buried near one of the building's cornerstones. With 2000 approaching in six months, the University desperately sought to locate the capsule to unearth it on its upcoming fiftieth anniversary, but it seemed to not be at any such cornerstone. "Geiger counters, backhoes, covert military maneuvers, even the Amazing Kreskin called in on behalf of the Premier, couldn't find it." Dawn laughed at her own joke. No one had a better sense of humor than Dawn. And the laughter gained traction with Jonah as she shared how most of the administration from 1950-51 was sleeping the big sleep now and no former students had come forward to reveal the capsule's undisclosed location. This news story was a bust.

"It's actually pretty funny," Jonah said, pushing his

hands into the tops of his thighs and smiling from the corner of his eyes. "Not finding it, I mean. Everyone loves a failed quest. Hell, we live in an ironic age where everyone stoops to glibness and sarcasm. No one's sincere anymore. This is the perfect symbol for our new millennium." He lowered his head, laughed into his shoulder (he seemed embarrassed by the sounds he made when chuckling), and then he told Dawn that ennui and irony were at the heart of her fiction (at least in the two or three stories she had then published), and that she should pursue her own authenticity through art, explore lesbianism in her work, that is if she is a lesbian—she didn't look like a lesbian, "you're too cute to be a lesbian, but you are one, aren't you?"

Dawn said she wasn't one, she was, well, queer, and there's a difference, but cute had nothing to do with it, and these were subtleties which he wouldn't be able to pick up on, and he said try me, and then leaned over and kissed her. She thought she should want to slap him, but she didn't really. Maybe it was the wine and the haze of white and red from the painting diffusing the room with a strange mellowness (a word she hated by the way, because it reminded her of Donovan, a fourth-rate Bob Dylan), but she embraced the word, the mood, and stared at King (the female dog), whose face was buried against her leg with one ear down, and the other flipped back. She wanted to straighten them out but was also digging the disjointedness. It was as if she were in a Picasso painting.

"I'm sorry, I shouldn't have. I've had too much to drink."

"That's not an excuse."

"I know—you're right."

"Just what *are* you selling?" Here her tone was meant to be accusatory, but came across flirty, as if a synapse misfired between intention and result. Many an accident like this led to good fiction on the page but in real life?

"I'm sorry—I—"

And then she kissed him back. Why? Three years later, she still wasn't sure, but this incident became the core scene of her working-class novel *Seeing Red, Feeling Blue* in which a young woman (modeled on Dawn) out of repressed anger at her mother's spacey inattentive-ness and embarrassment for her upper-class aspirations (modeled on a, well, a spacey, inattentive mother) sleeps with Mom's boyfriend (modeled on Jonah) and in the middle of his orgasm (she didn't have one), throws up on him—the ultimate act of aggression and diminish-ing of the self (hers and his). Deirdre, the lead character, isn't happy with Deirdre (she often refers to herself in the first-person novel in third person—just to fuck with the reader) and finds her confusing sexual orientation and sex itself dirty and thus acts out perversely to affirm her low status. The entire novel becomes a quest to find that damn time capsule buried in the 1950s, but Deirdre is really trying to free herself from her own restricted, passé notions of who she is and what she and any wom-an struggling with identity can be.

That night Dawn didn't sleep with Jonah or, thankful-ly, on any future night. They didn't have sex like Deirdre did, because Jonah was taken aback by Dawn's aggres-sion. To him she must have seemed but another version of Deanna trying to get her BA or buying a $1000 piece-of-shit painting, a woman moving beyond his control. Thus after the second kiss, Jonah slid not so subtly to the far side of the couch. The dog however remained at Dawn's side, snuggling against her leg.

"What? Suddenly you're scared of me?"

"Honestly? Yes." He said he had always been attracted to her, since the first time he met her at a downtown pastry store and bought her a chocolate croissant.

"You used to always buy me donuts and pastries."

"I was courting your Mom then. I was trying to impress you." He looked at the edges of his fingers. "I crossed a line tonight—but I just—I'm sorry."

Each time he apologized he was more and more sincere. She smiled slightly. "I'm sorry about King."

"You mean Lumpy Rutherford? Yeah." He rubbed the dog's ears. "You know, your mom doesn't even suspect that you're, well, you know? She doesn't—and—"

"My mom just doesn't listen that well. When she left Dad for you, she—she wouldn't hear me—how I felt—and then when he died—she—she wouldn't hear *him*. She played the wrong music at his goddamn funeral—Dad wanted Paul McCartney's 'Mull of Kintyre' and he had quit going to church, but she insisted on a full service and the minister pulled out some canned speech about the prodigal returning. It was bullshit."

Jonah reached for her hand. "Yeah. I was there. It was bullshit. John was a seeker, a questioner and he was way pissed at God for making him sick."

"Yeah."

The strange thing about Jonah, then and now, was

that she could talk to him. He got her.

"You want to go get some donuts?" He stood up.

She laughed. "Sure, in a minute or so."

"I do like the painting," he said. "From this angle anyway." He bent over, looking through the window of his legs at the wall and the white lines of uncertainty. "I think there might be someone else at the top of the hill. Mixed in the red."

"Oh, I see it, now, a woman," Dawn pointed.

"Yes."

"Oh, my God—"

"What?"

"She's wearing scarves," she said.

And they laughed.

"SHIT, SHIT, SHIT," MOM EXCLAIMED, SLAMMING A gloved hand on top of the steering wheel. "I left the painting at the apartment," she offered as way of exclamation for the outburst.

"The snow-storm thing? Mom, there's not space at my apartment for it."

"You don't have a wall?"

"Mom, I don't want that on my wall."

"I thought you liked it."

"On your wall, yes."

"Oh, shit." Now the door was left open, she said. Jonah had something of hers and she wasn't in control. It wasn't a clean break. Even in the watery shadows of the car, Dawn could see crease lines forming between Mom's eyebrows.

"If you want, we can go back and get it. I just don't

know how we're going to fit it in this car though. We could take a bus?"

"Shit, shit, shit."

"Mom, relax. You're going too fast." They were no longer on the Don Valley, but rushing through narrow streets, with 1930s homes and lights that occasionally glared all too brightly. Every now and then, they hit a strip of stores, white brick and lean glass, and then more homes with fading front porches and thin blue diamonds of light. "Let me drive, you're tense."

"I'm not tense," she yelled, nearly caroming like a billiard ball down a side street. A billboard above a three-story office building featured Mister Rogers in a sweater and smile and some message or other about being our neighbor, pass it on.

"Do you think he'll want to talk to me?"

"Who, Mister Rogers? He welcomes everyone."

"No, Jonah. God, is everything a joke to you?"

You know, the sweet, somewhat effeminate Mister Rogers was a marine in World War Two, a sniper, and killed fifty people? "That's why he always wears sweaters and long-sleeve shirts? His arms are covered in tats."

"Mister Rogers? No."

"Yes, he's a stone-cold killer—the Lee Harvey Oswald of children's programming, the Sirhan Sirhan of PBS. The Jack Ruby of—"

"Stop it—I want to talk seriously—" Deanna slid into the right lane and quickly cruised to a spot in front of a dry cleaner's and all-night variety store that happened to be closed. She let the car idle and looked at her gloved hands and then turned toward Dawn and wondered why everything she said had a twist to it.

"I'm teasing. It's an urban legend. Mr. Rogers never shot anyone. He's a vegetarian."

"There you go again with the jokes." Why was she such a smart ass? To Deanna it seemed like since Dawn was five she developed an all-knowing smirk too, like everything they teach in school about nation building and citizenship was a con. To play by the rules wouldn't get you anywhere. Her older sister Miriam was conned—she held doors open for people, excelled in school, and cried when a random bird hit one of their house's windows, sputtered on its back and then expired. Miriam was married now and expecting her first born in four months, but Dawn hung condom effigies and made fun of ions like Mr. Rogers.

"Icons, Mom."

"Whatever."

"That prof was a prick."

"Everyone else is always the problem, when are you going to—"

"Don't give me any platitudes, please."

"Platitudes? Now just listen—you're not going to dismiss what I have to say." At five it was just a smirk, but by the time she was nine, Dawn adopted a superior attitude to her own mother. It was as if there were a defining moment and Deanna remembered it clearly: that Christmas Dawn got a chess set from her father and beat Mom in thirty minutes; by the fourth game she beat her in twelve moves. After that, Dawn didn't ask for another match. Instead, her eyes soldered into a dark steel blue that said you can't take care of me, Mom. "From that moment you lost respect for me."

"I didn't—come on. Chess? Are you kidding? It's just a game."

Outside the car, bits of paper and Styrofoam cups whipped against the sidewalk and the barred glass of the variety store's front door.

"You had to help me with my papers for school—I know that. I'm not as smart as you, you know, but—" She had read *Seeing Red, Feeling Blue* two times and didn't understand all the anger and irony and the way Dawn's novel presented everyone as a huckster or hustler or someone who wanted to take advantage of someone else. Is there nothing, nothing that you find real? Mister Rogers cares about people. Mister Rogers *is real*, sacred. Two lights in a donut shop across the street flickered and then burst into a bright fluorescent glow.

"Mom, you don't get it."

And then Deanna slapped Dawn. It was hard and Dawn flinched with nettled pain. She couldn't remember Mom ever hitting her, not once as a kid. She believed in timeouts not corporal punishment.

"I don't *get it*. You don't think I know? I don't see?" How dare Dawn underestimate her mother. "You're going to tell me right now that in your purse there aren't three photographs of you topless? Jonah told me all about it two years ago. I don't *know*?" She gripped a hand tight on the wheel and looked out the window. The bits of paper and torn cups were still.

"You knew?—all this time—?"

If Dawn had been paying any attention, she would have noticed that the photographs weren't in Jonah's desk drawer but Deanna's. "I've had them for some time."

"How long?"

"What does it matter how long?—I had them." She shook her head and adjusted the scarf around her neck. "I know you didn't sleep with him, but did you have to go all *Girls Gone Wild*?"

Now Deanna was sounding like Dawn, using pop-culture references as adjectival phrases, ways to reduce complex human behavior to simple, moronic choices, and she didn't like the cutting irony—it was ugly.

"No. No." What possessed her that night to pose for those damn photographs? She wasn't sure. She wanted to feel dirty, she wanted to make him dirty, so she suggested, demanded the ritualized performance, and he reluctantly snapped the photos. It was a control game that got away from her. "I'm surprised he told you—"

He'd had one or two other indiscretions over the years but it was Jonah's moment with Dawn that made it so hard to reconcile. Maria was a desperate attempt to finalize the break, to force Deanna's hand, but that moment with Dawn is what really changed the course of Deanna and Jonah's life together. A line had been crossed and the two of them never trusted the same way again. "Write about that," Mom said, tersely, "instead of puking on someone. That's trendy. That's not real."

"The critics seemed to like it."

"I know you're capable of better, honey." The tone of Mom's voice became light again, like it was full of fabric softener, dissolving her disappointment with the world as if it were a stain that could be easily removed. She loosened her fingers on the wheel, shrugged, and looked at the blue lump of nylon filling the backseat. "Let's go get the painting."

"You sure?"

Deanna had never married Jonah—they had lived common-law for seven years, and preliminary talks with a Dundas Street lawyer were in Mom's favor. If Deanna left Jonah (she now no longer referred to him as her "possibly soon-to-be ex"), she was entitled to a fair share.

"So you're no longer interested in talking it out—?"

"Shit, shit, shit," she whispered into the steering wheel. "What am I going to do with all this fucking junk?"

Ossining, 1918

∾

A MAN STANDS, HANDS IN POCKETS, HEAD DOWN, glasses pinching his nose, shoulders sagging slightly, as he contemplates some mystery of living, some such uncertainty that drives all of us to wonder. Dressed in black, the man suggests a pursuit of hopeful inquiry. But those hands—in pockets—resonate a shyness before the world, a vague faraway awareness that there is so much that we are incapable of knowing. He's resigned to truth, committed to the painful journey of discovery.

Eighteen-year-old Jim Cagney wasn't quite sure why this painting by Thomas Eakins crowded his thoughts as the young catcher crouched behind home plate, knees sore and shin guards dotted with perforated chalk lines. Between pitches, Jim smacked a fist into the heart of his glove and adjusted the heavy mask smelling of wet leather. As he gave the signs, he wondered why the subject in the painting never takes off his glasses—Cagney certainly would if he were playing the part on stage.

Jim couldn't remember what pitch he had just called for so he went back to one, the fastball. The batter in prison grays grunted and missed the pitch breaking at the knees.

"Jim, you laughing at me?"

"Huh? No. I—uh—that thing fell off the table. Our pitcher's never done that."

"You haven't even said hi to me. I'm thinking you're getting kind of stuck up, Jimmy."

The batter lowered his hands on the bat's handle, and Jim suddenly registered the reedy voice with milkshake edges. Peter Hessling, Bootah, a kid who enjoyed hanging off the gutters of five-story buildings; Bootah, who at eighteen robbed a delivery truck, and then years after this game, 1926, would kill a cop for trying to apprehend him; Bootah, who even then Jim knew had the touch of the gutter that would help inform his later actorly life.

"You kept saying, 'Red.' Lots of fellas go by that nickname." It was only the second inning and Bootah was sixty pounds heavier than he was on the outside, back when they were fifteen and fistfighting.

"Remember when we used to call you Short Shit?"

"I hated that," Jim said.

Bootah smiled. "Well, hell, it's good to see you." The grin broadened. "Don't let me look bad in front of the fellas, huh? No more screwballs?"

Jim nodded.

"That your Pop in right field?"

It was. The Yorkville Nut Club, a group of 18- to 23-year-old ballplayers, occasionally barnstormed through the New York area. This week it was Ossining, north of the city, but a strange three-day virus had racked Manhattan and the club. Several key players were down with fever and nausea. The boys picked up four fathers to join their rowdy crew.

"Yeah, that's fucking weird." Bootah spat in front of the batter's box. "It's gone through the prison too." He rested the bat on his shoulder. "Your Pop's playing kind of shallow, ain't he?"

Jim agreed and set up on the far corner of the plate. "Fastball, outside," he winked.

Bootah extended his arms and smacked a comet over James's head. The ball caromed off the hard dirt with puffs of dust and rolled and rolled before the center fielder hit the relay man at second. Bootah was standing on third.

Jim gently whistled.

JIM DIDN'T GET ALONG WITH HIS POP. HIS FATHER operated a saloon, drank sixty shots a day while kibitzing with the customers, and paid the penalty many a morning, screaming at hellhounds. Jim himself would never become a drinker.

Rumors of Pop's dalliances—some of the women were married—echoed in the dusky streets outside their upstairs flat. Carolyn, Jim's mom, never let on that she knew, but now and then there was a terrific row. Most of the time, however, Carrie and everyone else just took to Jim's father. There was a glint as he spoke and he never hid his true self. A raconteur, Pop lacked reserve and played everything robust.

But he wasn't the kind of man to save money or think about tomorrow or to stand with hands in pockets, dwelling on uncertainties. Time was of no importance. Unlike the man in Eakins's portrait, no thin chains of a pocketwatch ever threaded through his vest.

"Jamesie-O, I never thought he could hit that pitch." Pop sat next to young Jim in the dugout. Lawes Field wasn't quite built yet—that was five years away. There were no grandstands for the prisoners to watch from, just random people in gray, leaning with the slight breeze, shielding eyes from the sharp sun. Behind were low hills, high barbwire fences, and turreted guards with machine guns. Pop repeated how he'd hate to be trapped in a place like this.

"Da, it's only seven innings. We're in the third."

"I know, Jim, I know." And then he started up with "Danny Boy," a sure sign that he was nervous.

Cagney breathed in, pounded his chest, and stretched his arms. "Mmm, feel that air. I tell you, feel that air."

The players next to him laughed. Jim dropped little touches of comedy whenever things got too serious.

"That guy on third base is one crazy sonuvabitch," Pop said, recounting how last inning to break up a double play Sonuvabitch cleated the team's second baseman.

"Yeah. It's Ty Cobb–style."

"Ty Cobb? More like gangland. Rat-a-tat-tat."

"Da—"

"Goddamn mental case." Pop wiped the corners of his mouth where spots of spittle formed. "Say, isn't that Will Carney?" He squinted in the direction of third. "Mike and Sharon's boy?"

Cagney and Carney had tangled a fair amount a few years back. Fighting for Jim wasn't something he sought out; it was just a part of street life. At thirteen, he even fought Grace Simek, but since she was a girl he didn't hit back. She landed a couple of beauties, however.

43

A few summers ago, Carney knifed a fella up pretty good and after a stint in reform school graduated to Sing Sing.

"That's him, ain't it?"

His widow's peak was but a faint reminder now. Carney's fuller face pulled his expressions downward, as if he were readying to take a punch on the chin. "Mmm. Feel that air, huh? Feel that air."

THE NEXT FEW INNINGS WERE PRETTY UNEVENTFUL, with each team scrapping out the odd hit but doing nothing with it, and the prisoners, coining themselves the "Mutual Welfare Club," were leading 3-2, and Jim, while swinging in the on-deck circle, drifted back to Eakins and the man who never seemed to take off his glasses or wind his watch. If Jim were thinking as hard as that man, he'd want to remove his glasses and rotate the hands on the watch, anything, to exert his existence on the world. But Eakins's subject was so patient. That's what drew Jim to the portrait. The contrasts. Jim was tired of waiting for whatever it was he was supposed to be waiting on.

Jim first saw the painting several summers ago when he turned thirteen and he and Grace had fought because she said he was getting awfully stuck up.

Jim always liked her. With her frizzy strawberry blonde hair shining different shades of sun, she belonged in a portrait. Grace was engaged with a world beyond their city block. If you couldn't jump rope, she showed you how to slide between arcing lines. If you couldn't write a clear composition for English, she offered stronger topic sentences, spiffier concrete details.

Anyway, Jim valued her friendship, appreciated her honesty, and a week after the fist fracas invited her to take the subway with him to the Metropolitan Museum of Art. There they saw the Eakins portrait, and Jimmy told her he admired dancing, baseball, poetry. He didn't want to be like his saloonkeeper father; Jim had a passion for words and colors that darted and dipped about the page or canvas.

"I just want to express myself," he said that afternoon at the Metropolitan. A catcher was kind of a flashy position, diving for pop flies behind the plate, throwing a runner out at second, but he never wanted to be one of those showoffs placing himself above everyone else. He reached for her hand. "I guess I was taking myself too seriously, becoming a regular swell head, and I appreciate you setting me straight."

Grace looked through his shoulder, her blue eyes dim in the museum's low light. "I've always liked you."

Two years later, all of Jim's self-assuredness disappeared. With most of the world at war, life had become confusing, as did Grace's illness. He didn't question God, but he couldn't understand why men killed other men and why Grace was afflicted with consumption. Often she retired to the "farm" for rest. And when she was home she sat by the front window, overlooking the street, no longer jumping in spinning arcs of rope. When Jim called on her, she'd sit in the dark, afraid to breathe on him.

Jim wished for the confidence of thirteen again. Sure, he still had street fights, but he felt like he was protecting a rep he no longer believed in. He looked down at the red and brown carpet.

"Jim, you have so much energy in everything you do." She smiled, a faint thin line. Grace spoke three languages—her parents were Jewish immigrants from Russia—but she admired Jim's ability to mimic others. His Yiddish was much better than hers, she confessed.

"*Ikh hob dikh lib,*" he said faintly.

"*Ikh visn, bubeleh,*" she said.

He laughed and as she turned away from the window she spoke of ancestral voices, splashes of light telling her it was time. She shrugged and wondered out loud if this were the secret of the Eakins painting. "You can't hold onto time." It's a game of jump rope without a beginning or end.

Jim stood silently. Children on the street filled the spaces between them. It was the last time Jim saw Grace. Two days later she was back in an upstate hospital. Six months after the spring baseball game with the prisoners, 1918, she died.

In the top of the sixth, Jim hit a homerun, a ball in the gap that roller-skated along the grass, his mind far away.

The live-ball era, and the game of baseball that Babe Ruth built, hadn't emerged yet. It was on the horizons.

In the bottom of the sixth, following a double and a walk, the prisoners had something going. With the score tied 3-3, their pitcher out of gas, Jim's father, a practitioner of a floating knuckleball, was now relieving. Before the alcohol, Pop had been a decent pitcher, earning the nickname Jimmy Steam. But now all he had left was chutzpah.

The first batter whiffed on four pitches that fluttered out of the strike zone. Carney was up next, his bushy eyebrows zippered into a long line as he spit tobacco on the edges of Jim's shoes. "That ain't no pitcher, that's one of them cake-eater dancers."

"You ever tried dancing, Beesack?" Prison officials had instructed the Nut Club not to talk to the convicts at any time—perhaps the Warden worried about the passing of shivs or contraband—but Cagney was needling Carney—catchers chatter like tommy guns.

"What did you call me?"

The first pitch floated like a butterfly sipping wild berries. Strike one.

"Can't hit what you can't see—right, Beesack?"

Carney hitched up his gray pants and clutched the bat tighter. Bootah, from the on-deck circle, motioned for Jim to ixnay on the wisecracks.

Earlier, Jim had noticed a hitch in Carney's batting approach. The big man got full extension by raising his left foot and striding toward the plate. But it was like putting your foot in a bucket and sometimes Carney missed the pail. Jim signaled for a fastball in on the hands. His father shook him off. Jim signaled again.

The change of pace clearly surprised Carney as he swung through the ball, twisting into a wrung out flag. As he unfurled, Carney cursed again, and the burly home-plate umpire told him that'll be enough, "it's Sunday for Chrissakes."

"What was that cake-eater shit you just pulled, Carney? A two-step, a waltz, or a rhumba?"

"Funny boy."

"Uh-huh."

"Well you're not, see."

"Gai kocken aufn yahm."

"What?"

Jim smiled. He had told Carney to go shit in the sea, but he wasn't about to translate the Yiddish. For the third pitch, Jim changed it up again. A knuckleball butterflied across the corner. Strike three. "So long, Beesack."

"Beesack, Beesack, goddamn Beesack," Carney grazed the top of Jimmy's left shoulder with a downward slope of his bat. The umpire shook the bat free, and Carney landed two lefts to Jimmy's head, one of them banging up against the cage of the catcher's mask, hurting his hand. Jimmy came out of his crouch and bull-rushed Carney, sending him sprawling to the ground, where he bloodied the prisoner's nose.

Bootah and James Senior were now also in the fracas, trying to restore order or prove their competing allegiances. Jim wasn't quite sure. His father may have landed a punch on Carney—Jim's mask was twisted around sideways so he couldn't tell for sure—and Bootah may have caught Jimmy's right shoulder with an overhand haymaker.

Head umpire Flaherty and five armed guards ordered both benches to remain seated and James Senior was looking up at turrets of machine guns. He crossed himself, and then the biggest of the guards escorted Carney—not so gently—to the prison infirmary. "Better get that nose looked at," he said.

"Why does he get to stay in the game?" Carney

huffed, blood dotting his prison grays.

"He's not bleeding."

"Bullshit."

"How's the hand? Looks like you may need a stitch or two."

"I'm fine, ya screw."

As they left, Jim glanced over at his father and shrugged. Carney's colorful exit, his final lines were full throttle street poetry. Jim adjusted his mask and felt bad for not having taken it off, but Carney just didn't give him a chance.

"Shit, Jimmy," Flaherty said, checking the indicator in his left hand: 0-2, one out. He adjusted it. "You know he's a head case. What did you get him going for?"

Jimmy said nothing.

"What's a Beesack anyway?"

"I don't know—I just made it up as we went along."

His father laughed but Jimmy didn't join in. He had picked on a guy who wasn't any challenge really and where was the victory in that? Jim wanted to stop fighting and rowing and making himself the big shot, but from the streets to the diamonds it seemed to follow him. Maybe he would never shake free of that image of himself—the feisty little Irishman, the territorial tough guy. Since fifteen, he saw himself as terrifically shy, gentle and soft-spoken, but that ten-eleven-twelve-thirteen-and-fourteen-year old kid kept crowding through, pushing aside the quieter Jim. Hell, it was hard to change peoples' perspectives of you, but all this fighting was something Grace would not have approved of.

"You okay, son?" His father noticed that Jim was favoring his left shoulder a little.

It was sore, but what Jim was really sore at was not living up to what he expected of himself.

"Damn—when I saw that boy come at you with a bat—" James looked at the ground. "Well, I couldn't just stand there." He shrugged. "Hell, Jamesie-O. I was afraid they was going to lock us all up and we'd never get out." His father glanced at the barbwire, the low hills, the machine guns. "Or maybe they'd open fire. Christ. I—I— and don't say, feel that air."

Jim laughed.

"You ready," asked Flaherty, pointing at Jim, and then the pitcher.

"Ready," his father sighed.

Bootah approached the plate and apologized for taking a swing at Jim. "I had to, Jimmy. I—the fellas here— they gotta think I'm with them."

"You were right to hit me."

"I knew you'd understand."

Jim stood at home plate, the mask on top of his head, his eyes pinched from its weight and the swirling dust and the fight and his own prickling of conscience. His hands rested in front of his thighs and he took a deep breath, trying to slow the world. Grace had seen lights, pockets of energy, telling her it was time. Jim wasn't sure what those lights held for him, but for a second he was in her halo, and now was a time for accounting, for Grace whose walk on earth was lightening, for Carney, who four years from now would be confined to an asylum for the criminally insane, for Bootah who on July 21, 1927, would be executed in the electric chair, and for his father, two other members of the Nut Club, and three prisoners that played on the field that day, who in just a few months would succumb to the influenza pandemic. In a moment of artistic clarity, Jim sensed all of this and mourned: for them, for himself, for all of us.

"Two outs." The umpire held up stubby fingers. "Jimmy, you ready?" He tapped the catcher's sore shoulder.

Jim adjusted his mask, took in a deep breath, and pounded his glove. "Ready," he said.

Carl D'Amato

∾

THE NEWS WAS HEAVY WITH THE STORY FROM CNN to Johnny Tenatas's local affiliate back in Northfield, Minnesota: Carl D'Amato, 47, a janitor at Peet Junior High in Cedar Falls, Iowa, had rescued two students whom a gunman, troubled fifteen-year-old Jimmy Destri, had taken into custody. Destri, according to reports, was a loner, had few friends, and often walked the halls with a fierce scowl on his face. He forced twelve-year-old Danica and thirteen-year-old Sydnee into a cramped AV closet in back of the media section to the library. Destri said that he was annoyed that none of the girls danced with him the last week at the annual winter dance. While Destri sulked and challenged the girls in shadows of closet, staff and students scrambled outside and waited for the police. D'Amato stayed in the school, knocked on the AV door, and according to Destri's sworn statement, told the kid he was loved, that he didn't have to do this. Five minutes passed and D'Amato's voice was "real relaxed like," said Destri. Eventually, the gunman came out. It was an air gun. The girls were all right.

Reporters snapped Carl's picture. He had a heavy face, the upper lip too small for the lower one's angry generosity. And his eyes were gray with dark troughs under them, making it look like he wore a mask. Johnny, who had been sitting at a Cedar Falls coffee shop for close to an hour, reading a Philip Roth novel and sipping Italian sodas, recognized the face in the newspaper sprawled on the table next to him. It was especially noticeable in the high cheekbones. D'Amato was Johnny's father.

Johnny hadn't seen him in nine years. He sipped more soda and tapped the packet of Camels resting next to his book. He wanted a smoke but it was too cold outside. Just what did D'Amato say for five minutes to Destri to gain access to him in the AV closet? And when did Johnny's father, Sol Tenatas, change his name? The street was gray with sky and snow flickered like caught lightning bugs.

For Johnny, memories of Dad were vague shimmers: lime-scented aftershave; two layers of flannel shirts billowing as he planted barbwire along the house's fencing to keep the deer out; buzzed hair and a dark river line at the back of his neck. Other memories weren't shimmers but hard flashes: the haze of alcohol that hovered in Dad's glassy eyes; the sandy stains on his T-shirts; crumpled radios, TVs, edges of coffee tables—items Dad had kicked or tossed in an effort to deflect anger away from wife and son. After school young Johnny gauged Dad's face to know what kind of a day it was going to be. If Dad wore sunglasses all was good—he was happy with drink. If his lower lip jutted above his thin upper one then anything could happen.

Three days ago when Mom first saw Dad on TV she

gasped, "It's him. It's, my God, it's—" She had slipped out of her office secretary clothes—pantsuit and flats—and wore bleach-stained sweats that bunched at her elbows and knees. Her forearms, dotted with odd, lake-like liver spots, were folded tight. Johnny couldn't believe it either. Dad's eyes weren't creased with fatigue as they were nine-ten years ago, but the lines under them were deeper. They looked like charcoal stripes.

Compared to his father, Johnny had never done anything heroic. Only eighteen, he was just readying to start college and, except for his father's abandonment, life had been uneventful. Johnny volunteered at the Western Home twice a week, attending to the needs of the elderly; earned okay grades at school, B's mainly; and played varsity soccer. Dad rescued two kids from a gunman.

"It was an air gun," Mom corrected, her eyes darkening.

"Mom—it looked like a real gun. Besides—he—I wonder what he told him?"

"Huh?"

"Destri. The kid with the gun, *air* gun. The news reports said that Dad told him he was loved. Loved, you know? They talked for five minutes—"

Mom bit at her lower lip. "'Loved'? Where was all that wonderful love for us, huh?" Just then the smoke alarm screamed and Mom rushed to the kitchen and switched the fan on above the range. She said something about the pizza being a little tanned.

The news story was full of absurd details and complexities. Above and below the commentator's analysis and the noisy wash of the fan Johnny heard the sharp, blunted tones of his mother, saying how they hadn't seen him in nine years, no child support in six of them, and now he was even living in a different state. Damn dead beat. "Some hero."

Mom continued rallying Johnny to her anger, but the fan above the range had progressed from a noisy wash to a metallic rattle and he could no longer hear her. Maybe, we redefine ourselves every moment in the choices we make, Johnny figured. The dad of his past had become in one moment a better man than he had ever been. The dampened faces of the two rescued girls, Danica and Sydnee, told Johnny how much his father was appreciated. According to newspaper reports, both families thanked Mr. D'Amato and invited him over for dinner. Danica's parents were expecting a fifth child and they had asked Mr. D'Amato to be the child's godfather.

Now, as the last of Johnny's soda glasses were empty, he crunched on a small pebble of ice, tapped his cigarettes, and glanced at his watch. Three o'clock. Peet Junior High was just around the corner from the coffee shop, about a ten-minute walk, and classes were dismissed at 3:03. D'Amato? Where did Dad come up with that one? There are no D'Amatos in any limbs to the Tenatas family tree. Outside, the gray had now darkened; the sky asphalt.

He wasn't sure of what he was going to do. He had taken the four-hour bus ride from Minnesota to Iowa, hopped in a cab to Cedar Falls, and desired a meeting with his father to learn what Dad had said to another kid that he should have been saying to his own son.

The very journey was sort of sentimental, melodramatic even, but Johnny felt compelled to take it, to hear his father's story, and maybe make him listen to the son's story.

He wanted to diminish his father, the "hero." He wanted to press Dad on his past behaviors, scold him for leaving. The word *love* was never spoken in the Tenatas home. Johnny couldn't remember being kissed or hugged by Mom or Dad. One Christmas, Dad got Johnny a pedal car to ride around the block but couldn't figure out how to put the damn thing together so it sat in the garage for six weeks until Uncle Vic, a fellow drinking buddy in dark sunglasses, brought over a bigger toolbox. Vic often smelled of stale socks and beer. He never wore deodorant. Didn't believe in it. Causes cancer, he once said. Six weeks. Car parts—sprockets, chains, and steering wheel—were scattered in the garage's sawdust. What if Dad had waited six weeks before talking to Destri?

Johnny picked up his pack of smokes, the Roth book, and tapered his knit cap over forehead and eyebrows. He thanked the girl behind the counter for the sodas and rubbed an eyebrow's edge and sighed deeply. Earlier in the week he had tried to contact his father but the number was unlisted. Johnny left messages at the school for D'Amato the janitor, but his calls were never returned.

Johnny cupped his hands into the crevices of his jacket—he'd forgotten to bring gloves—and stumbled into the cold. He immediately lit a cigarette while his shoes nubbed at salt and ice on the sidewalk. He had left a Post-it on the kitchen fridge for Mom, telling her he was skipping school and heading to Cedar Falls despite the fact that she didn't want him to have any contact with Dad. Last night she talked about suing Dad's ass and getting a lawyer all over him like rabbis and the NAACP at Mel Gibson's house. Mom's quirky sense of humor bubbled out whenever she got mad. What pithy punch line might she toss his way once he returned home? He didn't own a credit card; he didn't even have a toothbrush, a backpack, or a change of clothes—he'd forgotten all that. All he had was a return bus ticket, a paperback, and after a fifteen-dollar cab ride and six dollars of sodas, forty-five dollars—enough for a motel, maybe. Maybe he was walking too light.

When Johnny arrived at the school the sky's color had changed from asphalt gray to blacktop. Cars whooshed by, the streets thudding with heavy tires, and students, glittering in their ribbony scarves and bright winter coats, boarded busses and waited to be picked up by parents. The school itself was a low rectangle, probably built in the '60s, Johnny reasoned, when architectural design was very functional. On a niche in the school's brick was a crisp blue-ribbon placard, celebrating Peet's recent academic achievements. Johnny threw away his cigarette and entered the building.

He hoped to discover Dad working in a hall or room and catch a genuine response. But upon taking three, maybe four steps, a man and a woman from behind the series of glass panels to the main office gathered around him, their brittle ID tags flashing. He should have figured on that, what with the recent air gun/hostage incident. The woman was small with padded shoulders, an upturned nose, and eyes that were like hardened coins.

The man had a heavy face and his chunky tie was tucked into the folds of his buttoned shirt. Both were pleasant. The man was younger than the secretary and he asked Johnny what he wanted.

Johnny didn't look like a junior high student. He couldn't just slide by and meld into the muted blues and neutral grays of the school's walls and lockers. "I'm here to see my dad," he blurted, looking at his shoes and losing the battle to make eye contact. His jacket was unzipped. They could see he was unarmed. "Carl D'Amato."

Several minutes passed and Johnny didn't care much for the hard chair so he sat on its edge, trying to get comfortable, trying to keep his legs from falling asleep. He was tired of waiting. He had to see his father and give him hell for leaving years ago. A hero? Please.

The office was brightly lit, but the floor needed to be mopped—it was spackled with gray snow, and the clock to the right would occasionally tap loudly as the needle seemed to stick before moving to the next minute. The secretary smiled in Johnny's direction and asked if he had read the story about Carl. He had.

More minutes passed and then his father arrived. He wore green Dickies and a crisp shirt with little puffed tents on the shoulders. His shoes looked old, too old for the shirt. Dad nodded to the vice principal who in turn nodded back before retreating into his office. The secretary returned to sorting papers and filing notes. "Hey, Johnny." There was a catch to Dad's voice.

"Hey." Johnny didn't look up. His hands rested on his knees. "I heard about you on the news."

"Yeah. That's something, huh?"

"It's something."

His father suggested they talk in his office and motioned Johnny to follow. The blue halls were warm yet track lights glared violently off the floor's tile. They passed a large green trash bin on wheels with a towel on one of its handles. "I was in the middle of something," Carl said. Mice or squirrels, most probably, had sifted in between the drop ceiling and the ceiling and chewed wires. Dad had spliced the broken ends of bare wires back together.

"Cool," Johnny said, absently.

"You need to brush your teeth," his father said. "Your breath stinks."

The edges of Johnny's face burned. "Well—"

"Smells like you were in a barn."

"I brought deodorant—" He wanted to kick himself. Why did Dad always have this hold over him, this ability to make him feel small?

His father opened his office door. It was really a converted closet with cinder walls, a small desk, and rolls of cleanser under a rust-stained sink. Johnny was directed to sit down. A furnace duct to his left chugged as they sat across from each other.

"How you doing in school?"

Johnny could hardly make out his father's words. The furnace's chug seemed to drag the words out of the room.

"Okay." He was getting B's; a C in economics.

"In what?"

"Economics."

"Oh." His father shrugged. Math and sciences were

59

what mattered—that's where the jobs were.

"I prefer English and history." Actually, Johnny wanted to become an architect.

"What?"

"English—"

"Oh. Arty stuff." He smirked. "Like I said. Math and sciences."

"What?" Johnny heard him. He was just getting even for Dad's diminishing comments. Johnny shifted and knocked up against the desk's edge. "You remember the car with the pedals?"

"What?"

"The one with the pedals that you didn't build for six weeks? The one you got me for Christmas. It was Christmas, Dad. Six weeks."

"Oh, for Crissakes, Johnny. Is that what *this* is about? Where were you going to drive it—there was snow on the fucking ground—Mom wanted to get you the car, not me."

"What did you say to that kid, the shooter?"

His father leaned back and waited for a break in the chug of the furnace. "I told him there would be better days, I told him it's going to get better."

Johnny nodded, smiling slightly. "But you talked for five minutes—"

"What?"

"You talked for five minutes—"

"Well that's between me and him. It's private."

Johnny didn't know what to say, and both listened to the furnace.

And then his father spoke. At first, he said, he felt

he was acting, trying to say the right things to save the girls, but as he listened to Destri he was no longer acting. It wasn't so much the words themselves that mattered, but the emotion behind the words, the sincerity, that's what Destri was responding to from Carl. "Frankly, I can't remember what all I said. Something about logarithms and not having any girlfriends. I told him I don't have any either." His father apologetically shrugged and opened a desk drawer. He offered Johnny a leftover sub sandwich. "You hungry?"

Johnny was. "No, I'm good."

"I got that ceiling still to do—" He opened a prescription bottle and swallowed a white pill. Blood pressure. No big deal.

"That furnace is loud—"

"I'm sorry I messed up your life. Is that what you want from me?"

"No. I—I—"

"I'm not that person any more—"

"I know."

"I really got to get back to that ceiling—the squirrels?"

"Okay, sure."

"Look, I—I—damn, this furnace is loud." He laughed and Johnny joined in. "Let's do lunch tomorrow. We can talk longer. I'm a little off guard, here."

"Sounds good."

Carl rummaged through the desk drawer. "And even if you aren't hungry, at least take a few breath mints, huh?" He tossed Johnny the packet.

AFTERWARD, JOHNNY WANDERED THE STREETS OF Cedar Falls for two hours. He bought a Whopper for dinner, drank water to save money, and slouched aimlessly under shadows of an overpass. What was it he wanted? His father apologized, hadn't he, albeit half-heartedly but he had apologized. Johnny was dissatisfied with everything and wasn't even sure he wanted to meet for lunch tomorrow.

His feet felt heavy as if they were caked with hardened mud. The back of his knees, the corners in his arms, and the round fleshy part of his shoulders hurt with every step. Once he emerged from the overpass, he saw the red slash of a church.

The church doors were unlocked. Johnny's eyes adjusted to the darkness. He smelled candles and old sweaters and then slowly climbed carpeted steps to a balcony to lie down. It was cold in the balcony, probably because the heat in the church was set to a lower temperature to save money. As dry mud cracked from his upper back and arms, Johnny lay in the pew and studied the ceiling. It was darker than the backs of the pews and he thought maybe he saw chains. With dry, heavy eyelids, Johnny prayed for twenty minutes, then stared upward and found himself slipping, falling into a black lake.

"HEY, YOU CAN'T SLEEP HERE."

He blinked his eyes, momentarily thinking he was back in his bedroom, but when he didn't sense a pillow under him, he was confused, and the voice wasn't Mom's. The church. The darkness was lighter now and he could make out the stained-glass windows: fountains with jets of water. Over his head dangled a light fixture that resembled a giant goblet suspended with heavy chains. Mud fell from his eyes and eyebrows.

"You okay?" Parachuted by black hair, hovered the face of a girl. It was a pretty face: thin eyebrows, dark eyes, a high forehead. Her name was Claire.

"I'm sorry, Claire? Claire. I, what time is it?"

She was a big girl. Wide in the hips and chest and her upper arms were sturdy, strong, like maybe she lifted hay or something. He smiled. The edges of his lips still hurt.

It was after 9:30.

Claire handed him a cup of hot chocolate. "I thought you might like this."

"Thanks." He sipped it. It was rich and burned going down, which felt great. "I'm sorry. I just planned to close my eyes for a minute."

"That's okay." She picked at the book that crested from the open lip of his unzipped jacket. "Philip Roth, huh?" She liked some of his writing, but not *that* novel. "Terrible. Sexist. A woman freezes to death—"

"Well thanks for giving away the plot."

"Oh, God." She covered her mouth. Her teeth were very bright. "I'm terrible at that. 'Spoiler Alert.' Someone should tattoo that on my forehead. Too-much-information Claire. That's me."

He laughed and between sips of hot chocolate they made quick introductions: she was twenty-five, a grad student at the University of Northern Iowa, had taken a Roth seminar with Professor Julie Husband, and worked late afternoons and evenings at the church, caring for the parking lot, making sure the snow was blown clear. She also cleaned up the pews and polished floors too.

He told her he was just visiting and felt the urge to pray. "It happens."

"Yeah, it does." She smiled, her upper lip a chocolate mustache. "Why don't you come downstairs? It's cold up here."

"I thought I could be anonymous. That's why I came up here. I must have known all along that I was going to take a power nap." He chuckled. Power nap. He had been out for three hours.

Downstairs, the fellowship hall was a small meeting room with a quilt on a far wall, hard metal chairs by a fireplace, and three rectangular tables pushed against a kitchen nook. The room's walls were cinder blocks and it was very warm. The furnace was next door, she said. Outside the fellowship windows, streetlights gleamed and the parking lot resembled a pond that Johnny could skate on.

"So, you go to UNI?"

No. He told her he was from Minnesota, just visiting. "My dad's that guy that rescued those kids from the shooter—" Unlike his mother he didn't make a point of mentioning that the weapon was a lowly air gun.

"The newspapers didn't say anything about him having a family."

"No—no. I haven't seen him in nine years." He shrugged and suddenly found himself with a mouth full of tears.

Claire said it was okay and directed him to one of the long tables. Her hand on his shoulder was warm and full of kindness. He sat back, his head resting against cinder blocks. The furnace hushed. "I'm all on edge." He leaned forward and told her about the meeting with his father, how he wanted to punish him but felt belittled instead. He even mentioned the breath mints.

"I'm sorry," she said.

"I don't know what I wanted. Maybe I wanted him to hit me. Like it would feel good, like it was an affirmation that I existed for him, you know?"

She nodded.

"I don't know how to relate to him."

She looked at her fingers. "The hot chocolate's cold. You want another?"

"I'm kind of hungry. You got an egg you can fry up or something?"

"Yeah. In the kitchen."

"I'm sorry to ask. I haven't much money." He paused. "You don't even have a suitcase or a backpack—and—"

"—or a toothbrush." He shook his head. "Boy, it sure is nice and warm in here."

"The furnace." She touched the wall behind him. "Come on, let's get something to eat."

THE NEXT DAY AT CLAIRE'S URGING JOHNNY CALLED the school and confirmed his lunchtime appointment with his father. The night before, Claire let Johnny sleep over at the church—there was a mattress and old sleeping bags in the furnace room.

Now she was saying goodbye as Johnny's father stood waiting in front of the school, hands crammed in his pockets. Instead of Dickies he wore a double set of cornflower flannels. The collars were faded, and the fabric looked warm, relaxed. As Johnny left the car, he wanted to linger with Claire. But her head was slightly bent, her eyes elsewhere.

"You need to shower," Dad said, looking over his son who wore yesterday's clothes: blue jeans, a Rancid sweatshirt, and an unzipped jacket.

"Yeah, I know. I couldn't exactly afford a hotel, Dad."

"How about some deodorant?"

"I have deodorant, Dad. I told you that."

His dad shook his head. "Well, I have a toothbrush you can have."

They walked down the hall to the utility closet.

Dad handed Johnny a sub. "I didn't know what you liked—I hope you like Italian."

Johnny said that would be just fine, and then Dad ambled like an actor in a Western to the filing cabinet. The door opened with a creased yawn, and Dad tossed Johnny an unopened toothbrush.

As they sat down, chairs scraped the floor. They ate for several minutes before speaking. The conversation contoured down many different topics—who's that girl who dropped you off?—she's cute—how's your mother?—does she still not know how to make Jell-O?—hers always had a rubbery texture; she got bored stirring it—anyway, I don't blame her if she wants to sue me, I guess—and then Dad talked just a little bit about Jimmy Destri. The kid's father was an alcoholic. His mother a waitress at a low-fi bar in Waterloo. She often turned tricks in the parking lot for extra coin. "Seriously." Dad

shrugged. Jimmy was undergoing psychological evaluation and had asked to see Carl. He was thinking of visiting the kid. "Can you imagine that?"

"That's pretty cool."

He nodded. They finished their sandwiches and
tossed wax paper into a wastebasket. Johnny needed two
tosses and his father reminded him of this fact by mor-
phing into John Wayne of *Rio Bravo*. "Took ya two," he
said as Sheriff John T. Chance.

It wasn't like they were trying to shoot flying dyna-
mite or anything. Well, maybe Carl was, with words. No
matter.

The past never came up, at least not directly. Dad offered no explanations. He did say that he had been sober
for seven years and since the doctor had found a small
spot on a lung, three years ago, had quit smoking.

Johnny slightly smiled. He enjoyed their conversation, but halfway into it he knew he wouldn't find
closure, an answer for why his father abandoned him.
Rationally, Johnny didn't really think closure could be
achieved in one short conversation, but emotionally he
wanted it nonetheless.

"You need any money for the trip home?"

"No, no. I've got enough."

Dad placed tired hands on his knees. Some of his
fingernails were hard and yellow with age. He seemed
relieved about the money thing.

"Dad, why did you choose the name D'Amato?"

"Carl D'Amato. Not just the last name." He laughed.
"Boy, that's a story."

Before Johnny was born, Sol Tenatas worked con-

struction, helping maintain weather-beaten high-
ways and bridges in southern Iowa. Carl D'Amato was
the foreman of their road gang, a nice guy who died
too young, anyway, he was real nice, knew everyone's
names, likes and dislikes. He wasn't a big guy—soft spoken, really—but he never said a bad word about nobody
and when he spoke it was like parables. "Mysteries, you
know? He used to tell this one story about squirrels.
'You see, squirrels,' he'd say, 'aren't very smart. No sir.
They're digging up, uncovering, and burying acorns all
day because they can't remember where they put them.
Short attention span or no attention span or something,
so they bury way more acorns than they need, but no
squirrel ever went hungry because they're always finding some other poor schmuck's acorns.' Then he'd smile,
this big cat-like smile. 'There, boys,' he'd say, 'therein lies
the secret to life.' He never did tell us what the secret was
but it was somewhere in that story." Dad wiped the corners of his mouth. He had wanted to name Johnny after
the foreman but Mom vetoed it. Johnny was named after
an uncle. "Well, actually, your uncle's name was Sean.
But you know your mother—that's more of her quirky
sense of humor."

"I never see many squirrels in the winter," Johnny
said.

"They hibernate. Short term, I think. But they're
around."

"Yeah."

LATER THAT NIGHT AS JOHNNY WAITED FOR A
Greyhound out of downtown Waterloo, he thought

he saw a squirrel skittering along the lower casement windows of the library across the street. Its tail was puffed like a raccoon, but it wasn't a squirrel. It was a small cat. The cat moved closer to the warmth of the window's glass and apparently was staring out into the street's dull glimmer. Above the bus station's neon glow, a streetlamp flickered intermittently. White, then nothing. White—

Johnny wasn't sure for how long that light could hold a charge.

The Hermit Finds Solace

⁓

PERHAPS THE ANTI-SOCIAL BEHAVIOR STARTED for Gray Davies when he was a kid, tearing up the flowers in a neighbor's yard, lofting them across the fence between the two houses, and laughing as if he were a character in a Warner Brothers cartoon. Or perhaps it was fifth grade when he wandered the halls of a hotel, dumping teammates' blankets and pillows, hockey skates and pucks, down a stairwell, shouting "he shoots, he scores!" In middle school Gray quit trying to be funny and found comfort in hanging with a couple of burnouts and listening to Doors records. When Ryan Fraser joined their group in high school he and Gray became bodybuilding partners and slammed weights in the basement of Ryan's house, smoked dope, and read offbeat books like *Bonjour Tristesse* and the *Bhagavad Gita*. In college Gray drifted further into angst and alienation, reading for hours at the library—observing others—adopting a mood of solitude before possibly re-emerging into the world. Periodically, while riding the campus bus, he'd flip the finger to a young female student. "I didn't ask her to smile at me." Now, a college senior, he sat in Dean Flanagan's office, the Dean wondering why Gray had *yet* to pick up his mail.

"What's the idea?" Finn Flanagan huffed, shirttails dipped out, a sleeve cuffed past his elbow. "I have been trying to contact you for over seven weeks now." He hadn't seen Gray all of last semester, at none of the colloquia for honors students. "These are all my letters." Finn tossed them at an awkward angle in front of Gray who sat in a hard plastic chair and nodded. Six unopened letters were joined by a lava spread of seven months' worth of direct mailers, campus brochures, and credit card offers. "Don't you ever clear out your mailbox?"

"Apparently not. I don't have a key." Gray looked beyond the wide office window. A pine tree swayed gently on a small hill. The branches in the middle and top were much thicker than the winnowed ones near the bottom.

"You weren't issued a key?"

"I didn't want one."

"You didn't?"

"No." He shrugged and sat back. "It's too much hassle. I didn't ask for a key."

"Every student has a key."

"Not this one."

Dr. Flanagan huffed again sharply, his face puffed Wheaties, and propped his hands atop his walnut desk. "You deliberately don't want to be a part of the university community." Didn't he realize that being an honors student was a privilege and part of the responsibilities of the position involves attending certain functions, such as the J. M. S. Careless Lecture Series. Each monthly lecture included the work of scholars and students. This week, Careless himself was visiting Trent University, discussing his experiences in World War II.

"Attendance isn't required," Gray said.

"No. But it is expected."

"Then it's required."

"No. Not quite." Flanagan's face looked soggy now, the cheeks no longer puffed but falling, pulled down by defeat. "I'm insulted that you didn't get your mail." He opened one of the letters that he had written and read aloud. Finn had a very theatrical voice, scoring key turns of phrase and punching up the right words. In the letter he reminded Davies of the perks of being an honors student, how these lectures professionalized him.

"I don't care for the lecture series. I think it's elitist."

"Elitist?"

"Yeah." Why not invite the whole university and town to the series? Why close it off to honors students in English and History? "When Margaret Laurence visited Trent it wasn't a closed-door session. It was open to everyone: students, the community, the media."

"Margaret Laurence is a superstar."

"That too is an elitist position."

"Oh, come on. Grow up." Dr. Flanagan's eyes looked out the window, wondering, perhaps, what in the horizon line held Gray's attention.

"The leaves aren't even. They're odd-shaped. I find it striking."

Dr. Flanagan paused and rubbed his lips—perhaps he too found the tree striking. He waited another beat or two, rubbed his lower lip once again with an index finger and gave a narrow smile. "Gray, I'm trying to help you—'elitist'? Look at your thin goatee, dyed red so it won't match your natural hair color—that's not elitist?

You're a series of contradictions."

Gray shrugged absently. In his final film project for Professor O. S. Mitchell's class, Gray played a hermit: the incongruity in hair gave the lead an ill-fitted appearance, a marker of the marginalized.

"Maybe you're not cut out for university life."

"I'm not required to come to the lectures; I'm not required to get a key. I—"

"Well, will you get your goddamn mail out of my office? That I *require* of you."

"Certainly." It took Gray a few minutes to slide the lumpy lava into his backpack. When he was done, he thanked Dr. Flanagan for his time, congratulated him on a recent essay that appeared in *Modern Theatre*, and suggested next time he wanted to chat, call me at home. "I have an answering machine. I check that. I don't do mail."

"You read my essay?"

"Yeah. Sean O'Casey and the use of comic relief? You bet." Flanagan's point was that the playwright's comic sensibility increases tension, doesn't relieve it. "It was quite good. The language precise." He shrugged. "'Terrible state of chassis,'" Gray mumbled gently.

"Get out," Dr. Flanagan said quietly, a narrow smile returning to his crooked lips.

"Yes, sir," Gray said, even more quietly.

GRAY HAD NEVER BEEN IN LOVE AND HE WASN'T EVEN sure he ever loved his parents. His mom was the retreating type, reserved, and never said much in the way of the personal. She had a hard childhood—that's all he knew. Dad, a delivery driver, yelled most of the time, or snapped off the kitchen faucet or tossed pizza at the walls when he was frustrated, which was often. He used to smack Gray around until the bodybuilding leveled the strength between them, and now Gray hadn't seen his dad in five years. About love, Gray wasn't sure he wanted a relationship—he was going to remain free to do and pursue what he wanted, not get mired in compromises. And yet his sense of self was undergoing revision. He liked Mary Beth, a student in Mitchell's class. He often found himself thinking about her, the dark, almost blue-black hair, the mole near her left eyebrow, and the eyes that were sad and expressive. One time he bumped into her at a book sale in the basement of a church, and was at a loss for words. He seldom spoke to people, but he wanted to talk to her, and when she saw the William Irish book in his hands, she recommended that he pass on it—it's misogynist. Gray took her advice and got Margaret Atwood's *Surfacing* instead.

Strangely distracted, he had been vaguely thinking about all this, including "mail call" with Finn, as he and Ryan, the cameraman for his experimental film "The Hermit," were shooting scenes along Charlotte Street in Peterborough.

Gray, with a loose-fitting plastic bag over his head, recited the Lord's Prayer and sang blips from "O Canada" and the Sex Pistols's "God Save the Queen."

"What's that all about?" Ryan asked, laughing, while taking short drags off a king-size cigarette.

Gray shrugged. "Had to recite that propaganda every day at school. All the way through junior high." One

Jewish kid always left the room, refusing to participate. Gray wished he were as cool.

"You are cool," Ryan said.

But the film needed a moment of redemption. It had been ten days since Gray had met with Finn and maybe the dean was right, maybe Gray needed to confront his subterranean life. Maybe if cinema is life and life is cinema, as Jean-Luc Godard had argued, then Gray needed a counterpoint. The film's ending was too easy. "I might ask Mary Beth to be in this—"

"What?" Ryan took a long drag off his cig. Women were nothing but trouble. And Mary Beth was one of them fuddy-duddy feminists.

"She's not a fuddy-duddy," Gray said.

Now it was Ryan's turn to shrug. It was like a ritual between them, a secret, private language.

That night Gray worked on the storyboards in his small apartment, searching for a redemptive moment. He changed the title to "The Hermit Finds Solace." In the original script, the hermit swims naked in the Otonabee River. As he drifts farther and farther out, the camera cuts to an extreme wide angle, suggesting a surrender to despair. But suicide's been done, what with Kate Chopin's *The Awakening* and Bruce Dern's lone ocean float in the recent *Coming Home*. So in a re-write, the hermit crosses to the other side and there waiting for him is Eve, naked too. They don't talk. Language has disintegrated. Instead, with exaggerated hand gestures, they show each other postcards and adverts torn from glossy magazines. These images of modernity are pulled from huge shoeboxes, until Adam and Eve eventually discard the whole lot and wistfully smile as the film ends.

An overt homage to Jean-Luc Godard without being derivative, Mary Beth Ventura said the following morning at a downtown Zellers. "I like the ending, I do. But I don't do nude scenes." She took a sip of coffee from a mug the size of a soup bowl.

"Eve didn't have a sheet." Gray hated to compromise for his art. That's why he never asked students in class to team up with him on his projects. Ryan was the cameraman, but wasn't a student. Moreover, Ryan wasn't a meddler. He followed instructions, knew his role. He even joined Gray on several daring missions, like stealing dinner trays from the cafeteria last winter and using them as sleds for midnight slides on the hills behind Champlain College.

"I know why you want me in this movie."

"What?" Gray felt the edges of his face burning, especially around the eyes.

Her Croatian and Italian ancestry gave her a very exotic, Mediterranean look, she said. "With this nose, I'm not mainstream."

She didn't look Scottish, that's for sure, but he liked her face, her smile. Sometimes—in profile—it was so ordinary. She had a chin that was too small for her fleshy cheeks, a nose with two slight bumps in it, and ears that stuck out. But when she laughed, she was full of an affectionate and appreciative light.

"So, I'm goofy and gritty? That's why you want me in this film—"

"No—I don't have the words—I—"

"Well—" She liked his movie. She tapped her chin

and reached for a cold fry. Take the scene at the hotel where the father sits the family down to announce leaving Toronto for his job opportunity in Peterborough— that was brutal. "I mean, they're kids. Of course they don't want to move, but Dad expected too much, and when they didn't live up to his romanticized ideals and said what they felt—oh, boy—"

Oh, boy is right. Dad, in the film and in Gray's actual life, had called the oldest son Captain Selfish and slapped the youngest (Gray) across the mouth. Later at the hotel restaurant Dad ordered his meal, and one for his wife and daughter, but refused to order for the boys. "I don't order for Captain Selfish and his sidekick, Me, Me, Me." The waitress waited a beat and awkwardly asked the boys herself. They ordered hamburgers. "That's the kind of food I expect selfish people to eat," the father said. As Mary Beth made Gray relive these moments from the screenplay, he confessed with a shrug, "That really happened. But I don't want to talk about me."

"Why not?"

"I'll let the movies do my talking." He held up a finger. "Like Jean-Luc Godard said, 'the truth twenty-four frames a second.'"

"I'll do it," she said, her gray eyes filling with comical light. "The scene."

"If I knew quoting Godard would get you to say yes—"

"Just don't objectify me." And then she said something about Simone de Beauvoir, *The Second Sex*, and advertising images subjugating women. The Maidenform woman was just too much.

"I won't."

"And I don't want Ryan doing the shoot. I know he's your cameraman, but the guy kind of creeps me out."

Gray nodded, and surprisingly didn't feel guilty about tossing Ryan aside. "It'll be a closed set." He smiled. Ryan was kind of creepy. Last summer Ryan re-read the *Bhagavad Gita* and all he got out of it was how cool it would be to walk around with a big sword.

Maybe Gray should have felt more kindness toward his friend. He and Ryan had been weightlifting partners since tenth grade. The last two summers they had picked tobacco on a farm in Centreton. It was fifty miles from the city so they lived in a tent on the farmer's field, earning enough money to upgrade their weightlifting equipment, buying additional free weights and a variety of benches. Late at night in their tent, Ryan often spoke of their traveling to California after university, opening a gym on the beach, and picking up chicks. But their wrists, their bone structure was way too small, Gray wanted to counter. All the workouts and muscle drinks weren't ever going to change that.

Mary Beth pressed her hands against her upper thighs and then absently scratched a spot on her clavicle, hair falling over shoulders. She said the script was volatile, and then stabbed a fry in a puddle of ketchup.

"Success to crime," Gray said, which made absolutely no sense, but he loved quoting offbeat lines from the movies. Mary Beth took up the toast and they held their French fries aloft and crossed them like sword tips.

RYAN WASN'T TOO HAPPY ABOUT BEING BANNED FROM

the shoot and he was even less happy when a scene Mary Beth wrote was added to "The Hermit Finds Solace." They filmed it late on a Thursday, after the store closed. Gray donated $20 to Goodwill to get twenty minutes of shooting time. Ryan was surly during the shoot, a long-ashed cigarette drooping from his lower lip.

But Mary Beth's new scene was highly caffeinated, flavorful, and a hoot. For the scene, Mary Beth's Eve rummaged through snake lines of slinky scarves, while Gray's Adam smiled at her, and then she gave him an abrupt finger. "I didn't ask you to smile at me. Fuck you," she said, courtesy of an inter-title card that she held aloft like a ring card girl at a heavyweight bout.

"It's just a smile," he said.

"A smile is never just a smile." It implies a connection, a sense of shared feelings, and Eve didn't appreciate Adam crowding her space. She snapped the scarf over her left shoulder.

"Sometimes words fail us."

"Uh-huh."

"The smile was just an involuntary gesture. There was no agenda."

"Really? How's this for involuntary?" She pulled the scarf off her shoulder, roped it around his hips, and danced, singing about blue skies clearing up and insisting that they put on happy faces.

Gray followed her steps—they had choreographed it at her apartment two days before while Ryan was away—tipped back porkpie hats on their heads, painted themselves in colorful scarves, and spun about clothing racks. When the song ended they collapsed into shoulders before falling to the floor, laughing.

"I don't get it." Ryan tossed the hat on top of a clothes carousel. He lit another cigarette. "And the Ska fad won't last, you know," Ryan said.

Gray's artistic choices had never been questioned by Ryan before—this was new. "Aw, come on. It's killer."

"It's dumb," Ryan said.

Mary Beth looked away, no doubt sensing the personal slight. "I think it adds to the film's overall drive to mix and match apparently misaligned genres."

Ryan threw up his arms. "I don't even know what the hell you're talking about."

Gray nudged Ryan slightly, sending him stuttering forward. He almost lost his cigarette. "This from a guy who feeds beer to a dog?"

"You let a dog lap up beer?" Mary Beth asked.

"Sometimes," Ryan said. "I like to watch them stagger around. It's funny."

"No it's not," she said.

"I told you it wasn't, Dude," Gray said.

"Whatever."

Once Ryan had left, Mary Beth turned to Gray, a hand on her left hip. "Were you there when he fed beer to the dogs?"

"No—" Gray lied, but he wondered if she could tell.

In the parking lot, dusky under a dark sky, Mary Beth said she had a T'ai Chi class to get to. Maybe they could incorporate some of those steps into the final scene. He wasn't sure if she was inviting him to join her class. He wanted to offer to come along, but verbally stumbled. *The Apartment* was on TV tonight. He had to get home.

"Sure," she said. "*The Apartment*. A classic."

GRAY WASN'T EVEN SURE HE LIKED RYAN THE FIRST time they met. They had been paired up to dissect a mink in biology class and Ryan's breath was terrible, his teeth almost orange. And every now and then, he'd scrape at his back molars, look at the plaque under a fingernail, and then rub it on the sleeve of his shirt. But as they worked on the mink, they got to talking music and both liked obscure Stones tracks: Ryan was a big fan of "Connection" off *Between the Buttons* and Gray loved "Flight 505" off *Aftermath*. Something about setting a plane down in the sea was perversely funny and cool. Not long after that they started lifting weights together.

By contrast Gray liked Mary Beth the moment he saw her, strolling out of the library, her hair in a blue bandana, a peace chain glinting around her neck. He liked her the second time too. She probably didn't remember but when she was a sophomore Gray had spent a night with her. Well, it was with her and seven other people. They holed up in Mary Beth and Lonny Wilks's Water Street flat (Lonny was a philosophy student who became brief friends with Gray over a mutual appreciation for Jean Paul Sartre's *No Exit*). That night they smoked weed and watched VHS tapes of *Some Like it Hot* (Lon's choice) and *That Obscure Object of Desire* (Mary Beth's). Gray laughed and laughed at Jack Lemmon's Daphne voice and felt a little foolish for having so much fun. Later, just before dawn, they all walked down to the A&P. There, under bright track lights, Mary Beth danced with a chocolate cake, asking Gray to join her.

He couldn't shift his feet so she came over and nudged his legs along, as cake frosting slid against the underside of the plastic lid.

Mary Beth was no longer seeing Lon—he was in the Peace Corps now. So Gray saw her some mornings at the Pancake House, went with her to take in an Irish folk band, and once dropped in at Mother's Pizza where Ryan worked. Whenever his weightlifting pal visited Ryan usually piled Gray's pizzas with extra toppings— twice the ham and mushroom, double the cheese. But this one time there was no significant difference; if any- thing the toppings looked thinner, the cheese receding from the crust's edge.

Later that night, while readying to bench press 340 pounds, Gray asked about the mediocre pizza, and Ryan said something about the manager being there that day. He shrugged, absently smiled, and rubbed sweat off his wire-framed glasses. "Sorry, dude."

Sorry? Gray crushed chalk between his hands and clenched the bar, thumbs underneath, elbows in, spine loose. "You ready to spot me?"

"Yeah, yeah." Ryan hummed along to the Stones's "Rip this Joint." The edges of his mouth curled back a little. *Corporate rock dinosaurs?* The Stones? Can you believe that shit? He shrugged and exhaled sharply. "As near and dear to my heart as the CIA'? That's what she said. You know, I asked her to name five Stones songs off of one of the greatest rock albums of all time, *Exile on Main Street*, and she could name only two. So how the fuck can she judge, you know? Two songs and she's an expert?"

Gray slipped his fingers from the bar and flexed them. "I think you did it on purpose—"

"What?"

"The pizza. You're mad at her, you're mad at me."

"I'm not mad." Ryan pointed at the bar and the big wheels of weight. "You going to press that or not?"

"You can be decent to her—"

"Oh, I'm decent. I don't make fun of *her* music— fucking Blondie and the Cars."

Gray lifted the bar off the rack and extended it over his head, and maybe it was the argument with Ryan, or general fatigue and stress over finishing his film, but his arms shook, the bar wobbled with wrong intentions and anchored him to the bench.

Ryan's head peaked over the rack, his hair a greasy parachute. "What? Did you say something?"

"Can you give me a hand here?" Gray was buried.

"I didn't hear you say anything. Did you say something? I didn't hear anything. Just like you didn't say anything in front of her, huh?"

"What are you talking about?"

"The beer—You fed beer to dogs too, but you made me look bad." He shrugged and his head tilted left. Trying to impress her, but what about me?

"Get this thing off me, huh?"

Ryan turned up the music and sat on a different bench, looking at his fingers.

Gray couldn't slide the weights off the bar because he had tightened the collars. If he were alone he wouldn't have put on the collars. "Come on. Don't be an ass—" He could probably roll the bar across his stomach and abs but it would smart. Ryan had made Gray feel vulnerable and embarrassed and he hated that.

"Ass? Who's the one who never calls unless he needs a favor? Who's the one—"

"Okay, I'm sorry about the beer thing—"

"I bet. You've changed, man. Two songs off *Exile*—that's all she knew. But boy, has she got opinions—"

"Come on, man. I don't want to have to roll this bar—"

"You shouldn't have embarrassed me." Ryan's voice quavered slightly.

"You're right."

"You bet, I'm right." Ryan waited, did a phantom Charlie Watts fill with his hands, and then helped lift the heavy bar from Gray's chest, re-positioning it on the rack. Gray sat up, looked at his quivering arms, and felt anger pounding behind his eyes. Next time, he wouldn't put on the collars.

Ryan flipped the record over. "'Sweet Black Angel.' You know that was written in honor of Angela Davis," he said.

BESIDES GOING OUT TO EAT TOGETHER AND WATCHING art films, Gray helped Mary Beth edit her film, "The Teacher?" It was about a young woman who questions her chosen occupation after a horrific field experience in which the future teacher felt like a totalitarian dictator. All of her liberal values disappeared upon being confronted with an unruly group of at-risk kids. She told them to shut-up and copy down word-for-word the opening chapter to *To Kill a Mockingbird*. The film consisted of several long takes: all focused on an empty classroom, accompanied by a meditative voiceover that speculates on how social interaction re-shapes identity.

Since the pumping-iron incident, Gray and Ryan had hardly spoken.

By contrast, Gray and Mary Beth were good friends, but just friends. He was afraid to state his feelings from fear that she didn't feel the same.

One morning at the Pancake House, Mary Beth confessed that she added the "finger scene" to "The Hermit Finds Solace" because she had seen Gray flip a girl off who had smiled at him on the bus. It was last year, around Easter. Gray said he had been upset that day. His father sent him a birthday card in which he "disowned" him. In it his father wrote that the son had been so neglectful, so lacking in respect to the father, that the father was now denying ever having known the son. As he spoke to Mary Beth, he looked at his shoes.

"I was sitting at the back and I couldn't understand how you could do something like that."

"Yeah—I can't either. I was an ass."

And then he said he flipped the bird more than just that one time. Four, five, seventeen times. He had also given beer to dogs. He shrugged. She didn't shrug back.

FOR PROFESSOR MITCHELL'S FINAL TUTORIAL THE students screened each other's films in the basement of the library. Curiosity seekers, arty students from outside the class, were at the screening, and surprisingly so was Finn Flanagan. They sipped sodas and nibbled on crackers and pâté throughout the showings.

Production on the nude scene went well. Mary Beth filmed the long shots of Gray swimming against the current, cupping hands into cutting waves, and all close-ups of him in their shot/reverse shot scene. She said that he moved like a subtle cat. Gray had filmed Mary Beth tastefully. The nudity in her scene was much more suggested by what wasn't shown than by what was.

Although they hadn't spoken in several days, Ryan was there at the screening. He sat in a chair broken off from Gray's row.

The crowd had politely acknowledged each of the prior films, laughing at the appropriate moments, and waiting patiently as filmstrips stuttered in projectors or weak splices fell apart. One film even got caught in the gate and started to burn. But the response to Gray's film, a gurgling brush fire of noise, was much more robust. Gray was pleased but slightly embarrassed.

Twenty minutes later, after the last film was screened, Professor Mitchell thanked all for their work. And then from behind his back pulled out a film canister with a gold star on the lid, and said on this special occasion he wanted to give out an award for the best film, perhaps the best he'd ever seen in ten years of teaching at Trent, and called Gray to the front of the library's auditorium.

Initially, Gray hung back, unsure of what to do.

And then from the front of the room, he smiled, and wondered why the unusually cool fluorescent lights weren't warming his face. He sought to block the glare with a raised hand, but there really wasn't much glare. He nodded his head as if waving, and then handed the canister back to O. S. Thanks for the award, the gesture, but everyone deserves an award. This is about the creative crucible of art, about what happens when people create something out of a love for film, Gray said. Susan: your use of color and rhythmic editing was truly spectacular. Ivan: great use of claustrophobic close-ups to draw me into the drama. Wendy: admired your use of crosscutting, mixing up the timeline in a nonlinear fashion so that the love and the loss was all that more poignant. And Mary Beth. Wow. The voiceover, with no actors present, created an indelible mood of alienation and loss for the teacher. "All of the films were breathtaking." The award should be shared.

He paused, eyes wet, and his fellow students started a new brush fire of applause.

Professor Mitchell shook Gray's hand, and Dean Flanagan, now munching on a triangle-shaped cracker, smiled and said he had underestimated him.

"I'd like to try to make movies here," Gray said when asked by the dean about his future.

Dean Flanagan tucked in one of his shirttails. "Maybe we can find some grant money. Come to my office tomorrow some time. We'll brainstorm." He smiled. "I don't leave messages on bloody answering machines."

"Okay. Sure."

"Congratulations." And with that Finn mingled with some of the other students before making an early departure. Mary Beth squeezed the side of Gray's hand. It wasn't something a friend would do, but something somebody more than a friend would venture. "Where's Ryan?" she said.

"I don't know. I thought you knew." He scanned the

room, saw only clusters, but no one standing alone. Ryan would be alone.

"I think he was mad that you didn't take the award," she said.

"No. He was mad that—I—I should have mentioned him." He looked at the ground. He had congratulated all of the filmmakers, but none of the actors or crews. Ryan wasn't even a student in the class. He helped Gray with his films out of friendship. "I should have said something. Shit. A few lousy words." Ryan always lifted weights when he was upset. And even though they hadn't pumped iron since the regrettable to-spot-or-not-to-spot incident, maybe it was time to talk. "From here on in, I rag nobody," Gray quietly said, quoting another film.

"You know I would have kept the award?"

"Really?"

"Yeah." She kissed him on the cheek. "I'm not as nice a person as you."

"Yes, you are." And then he kissed her. Not on the forehead. The excitement of winning an award might have been the trigger, the emotional excuse, but he wanted to kiss her.

She smiled, and then suggested that he invite Ryan over to watch a movie at her apartment. She'll make appetizers.

He nodded, his mind drifting to Ryan's basement, the smell of chalk, sweat and steel, and the sounds of a distant beach that they would never walk upon, friends shifting under uneven sand and splashes of seagulls lapping at the waves.

Dead Flowers

MY SISTER MICHELLE LOVED THE SMELL OF alcohol.

As a young first or second grader, she couldn't label the smell as such, but she knew through its odor that Dad was in a good mood.

He wouldn't scream or toss our toys in a pyre on the living room rug and threaten to throw them away if we didn't clean up fast enough—wash the dishes, scrub the counters, pick up the basement.

Instead, Dad, wearing dark sunglasses, would vaguely smile, and slouch at the kitchen table, sipping from a perspiring beer bottle. "Meet your uncle Norris," he might say about a fellow milkman I had never met before. Norris too wore sunglasses.

Once Michelle, my brother Gary, and I were out of our school clothes and into our play clothes we were allowed to ride our bikes and get away.

I was nine or ten at the time, and I knew that sweaty alcohol smell. Bourbon and beer.

I tell you this story as a way to explain. As a way to understand. About a week ago my kid brother took a near overdose of heroin, pills, and vodka. He got dizzy and called Mom.

I somehow think it's all connected.

"YOU SHOULD GO SEE HIM," MY WIFE EMILY SAID WHEN we got Mom's phone call. Gary had taken the junk while at one of his favorite bars. He had been depressed since his wife died of cancer in November.

"I can't. At least not for a couple of weeks. You know that—"

I was in a community theatre production that opened up that August weekend. It runs next week too. I have a lead part. It's a comedy. The title doesn't matter.

"I know," she said, a slim smile on her lips that looked like cake crumbs. She patted my side. "He needs you."

"I'll go when it's done." I promised to take the kids to the Rock and Roll Hall of Fame in Cleveland as part of a summer trip. We could see my brother on the way.

Truth be told, I was glad I was in a play. I didn't want to see my brother right away. Last Christmas when I visited Mom in Toronto, Gary was avoiding me. I wasn't supposed to know about his wife's death. He was mad at me for some reason, and I was instructed by Mom not to call him. So it was awkward all around. I knew about Susan's death because I stumbled across it on the Internet. I was Googling my name, Griffin, trying to see if anyone said anything nice about my books. I'm a writer, after a fashion, some critics say. I've published a couple of detective novels and Griffin is sort of like Gary. Okay—it's not actually—but I was curious as to how he was—so I Googled his name and there was Susan's obit.

Anyway, it was Christmas and I'm standing in Mom's living room—she lives with Michelle in a small one-room flat—and through edges of silver tinsel that dotted the sunken windows I thought I saw my brother, lumbering along a gray stretch of Walmer Avenue. He wore a heavy plaid jacket, a black knit cap, and he rubbed at his beard with impatience. Anger hovered in his shoulders, and he stabbed at the ground with the balls of his Doc Martens. Did he want to see me? Did he want to punch me out? For the first time in my life I truly feared him.

The sky was cloudless. It hadn't snowed yet and everything was dirty and dim. Suddenly we caught each other's sightline. It was him, I'm pretty sure. He shrugged, gave a kind of wolf-like grin, and loped away, his side-to-side walk full of the same lack of purpose that my walk has.

"I think that was him," I mumbled.

"Huh?" Mom asked, her lower lip hanging loose, her arms gripping a walker. She had had a stroke two years ago, Labor Day.

"Gary," I said.

"Come on, now."

"Yeah, I saw him outside. I'm sure it was him."

"Come on, now."

I told Emily and Michelle about it after they returned from hitting the Boxing Day sales, and they were sure it was him. "He's kind of a control freak," Sis said.

WHEN WE WERE KIDS MY BROTHER WAS A DISRUPTIVE force. Michelle says it's like he's always gone through the world with a kind of corkscrew twist. No straight lines. Mom would take us to Eaton's and Gary stole bits of Play-Doh. He loved jamming the soft clumps in his pockets. The next day, he'd throw hardened specks at me.

He's three years younger than me, but when I was twelve I knew he could kick my ass.

When Gary was five, he ran into the neighbors' yards and broke up their lawn art, tossing metal petals and cracked plastic stems like bits of debris from an exploded airplane.

At fourteen, he stole tips off tables at restaurants.

And at sixteen, hating my father, he took up boxing. Gary has a license. He's fought over 160 rounds. He could train the likes of a George Chuvalo. Along with his boxing prowess, he has a black belt, two actually, and he throws knives. From fifty feet he can hit a target or put the blade within inches of your next step. Oh, and he rides a Harley and has had to lay it down four times. "Always on the left. The chrome's on the right," he says. Anything to be tough, to not be like my dad whom Gary thinks is weak.

It must have been early February before we started talking again—he was no longer mad at me, I guess. I had sent him a condolence card (I didn't care I wasn't supposed to know about Susan's death) and a book: Leonard Gardner's *Fat City* (he read it in an evening). I was in Toronto for a reading at Chapters, a big book chain, and later me and Gary sipped beers in his small apartment. That's when he told me that he loved me. "You're up there, man." He wore a T-shirt, jeans, and looked thinner than I remembered.

Bodybuilding equipment engulfed us. There was nowhere to sit. I was on the edge of a bench press. He was on some sort of pulley thing that worked your upper back. A framed photograph of Marilyn Monroe in jeans and bra adorned his wall. She was lying on a bench press, readying to push some weight. Steve Reeves, the first Hercules, was in a separate framed photograph, next to her.

"What are you talking about?"

"You're up there. You know that, don't you?" He smiled, pressing the tips of his fingers together.

"No. What do you mean?"

"You. Your family. Your two girls. They make me want to live."

I didn't know what to say. My face felt hot. "My girls like you a lot."

"Whatever."

"No, they do."

He said something about not being a good guy, about being fucked up, about still missing Susan. He hadn't been to work in months. He saw a therapist twice a week. And he was taking heroin on occasion. "I'm not a junkie. I'm not hooked. It just feels good."

I couldn't lecture him. He's thirty-five years old, but he could read my face.

"Don't worry. I'm not a junkie. Charlie Parker. There's a guy who had a taste for it. I'm just fucking around. I'm a poser-junkie."

He smiled a lupine, lopsided grin and moved quickly to the CD player in the corner of the room. We were listening to Hasil Adkins, some kind of hepped-up 1950s rockabilly cat who played guitar and drums simultaneously. The music was sloppy but had a libidinous undercurrent, which probably inspired my next comment.

"How can you ever invite a girl up here, man? Where would she sit?"

He laughed and asked if I wanted to hear Iggy and the Stooges. "No Fun" was still his favorite song. He had been playing it the other day while sitting on his balcony, fifteen stories above Kingston Road. The lake was beautiful he said, a deep blue, and the people next door were screaming at him.

"They didn't like Iggy?"

"No, man. No. I was sitting on my balcony. Literally sitting on it. You get me?"

"You mean, the railing?"

He touched the tip of his nose. "Bingo." He smiled. "Fifteen stories, baby."

"Don't worry, you won't hurt me," Denise Harms-Logan said. "I'm a big girl." She smiled and gently grabbed my left wrist. "Come on, let's work the scene again."

She was playing my wife in that comedy I was telling you about. Comedy? In the third act, I had to straddle and strangle her on a bed at the Howard Johnson's. Let's just say I felt awkward about the whole thing. I struggle with intimacy.

"You just put your hands there, gently by her neck, Griff," the director said. "Denise will control all the movement. She'll make it look like you're strangling her."

"Okay."

Denise smiled, kindness filling her eyes. "I won't get hurt. I promise." She had heavy bangs and auburn hair.

I said okay again, drifting into a Brando mumble. The director broke me of several bad habits, including eyes that won't stay focused, targeted. I'm shy so I don't always lock in on my fellow actors. With Denise I had got more comfortable, but just then I was drifting away again, aware of her as Denise and not just the character she played. Touching, hugging is really difficult for me. I've never hugged my brother. Maybe my sister and mom on a couple of holidays. Anyway, I had to touch Denise's shoulder in one scene—"it'll help you land your line," the director said. We held hands in the second act. We kissed in the third. I wanted to kiss her on the cheek, but the director said no, we're a married couple and it's New Years. But after opening night, my self-consciousness was diminishing. The audience laughed in places I didn't expect and Denise hugged me in the wings. I hugged back. "I bet you never thought you'd be that good, huh?"

I had no idea.

WHEN HE WAS FIFTEEN, MY BROTHER DEFIED MY FATHER. He was supposed to call at 10 p.m. for a ride home but didn't. From what I gathered, he stayed at Earl "Greasy" Walmsley's house. "Greasy" was a nickname Gary gave him. No one else dared call the kid from Pakistan "Greasy," but Gary pulled it off. They were weightlifting buddies and corners on the school football team.

Anyway, after hanging out at the beach and drinking beers, Gary slept it off at Earl's and came home the next day wearing someone else's baggy sweatshirt and bragging how he drank eighteen Molsons and got laid. He shoved the red, torn condom package at my father and laughed. Dad, who pulled our trousers down and smacked us with a strap when we were kids, said nothing. His left eye twitched slightly.

Later as I was finishing up my undergrad and preparing to attend Kansas State for an MA, my brother and I attended a hockey game at old Maple Leaf Gardens. On the streetcar ride back home, Gary sat at the edge of his seat and shouted, "Greasy's dead."

"What?"

Hours before, we had been laughing, enjoying the game. The Leafs had rallied in the third period to tie 3-3. No one scored in OT and there were no shootouts back then.

"Greasy."

"Earl?"

"He's dead," he shouted. "Dead." Several people in adjacent seats turned to us. I listened for the hiss and ding of the streetcar but couldn't find it. Greasy had washed up on the beach. Murdered. He was twenty-one.

"Who'd want to kill Earl?"

"He's dead," my brother repeated. "Dead."

OUR CONVERSATIONS ALWAYS WENT THAT WAY. RARELY linear. My brother's logic was baffling to say the least. All life's a lie, so why tell the truth? If the truth is what is, then do what you want. He often quoted something and turned it back on itself. "Ask not what your country can do for you. Ask for all you can fuckin' get."

My dad's kind of the same way. Except he makes jokes. If the checker tells him to "have a nice day," my dad jumps in with a loud, blustery, "Don't tell me what kind of a day to have."

And my poor sister. When she was twelve, Dad loved to embarrass her. "Hey, honey, do you need any of these?" he'd ask, holding up a box of Kotex. It wasn't funny then, and it pains me to recall it now.

So, when I heard my brother had taken some pills, heroin, and vodka, and that my mother had called 911, and the police, EMT, and fire trucks were sent to his apartment, I didn't want to get dragged into the drama. At least not yet. I wanted him to be okay. I love him and all that kind of stuff, but when my sister got to his apartment and found out the call had been canceled and he was nowhere to be found, I was glad to live in the Midwest, to be that far away, and in a play, a comedy, as I told you.

I felt safe, in Iowa.

When I was nineteen, my brother was institutionalized for nine months. He had tried to hang himself after taking heavy drugs and delving in the black arts. I only visited him once at the hospital's sequestered ward. There were eccentric people there that knew stuff like all the lines to *King Lear* or could rattle off in some kind of hallucinated reverie the numbers to pi in reverse order. I mean that's impossible to do. Pi is infinite. So how could you even start from the end? But this one older man was pretty convincing. But I digress. I can't quite remember the smell of the place. It wasn't soothing like alcohol. It was something else. It smelled of ammonia, and relief. My brother was no longer around.

My sister and I ate meals without Gary randomly tossing them in the backyard. He did that. Lift weights to the Rolling Stones—it was always the Stones—and scream as if the house were falling. He liked obscure tracks and played them over and over: "Fingerprint File," "Jigsaw Puzzle," and "Dead Flowers." The latter he sang along to in an exaggerated country twang. Anyway, following the rattled harangue of iron bars, Gary on occasion would lope upstairs and toss Michelle's meal.

By then my parents were divorced and Mom, her lower lip trembling, didn't say much. She couldn't even utter a "come on, now."

My bro's gesture, the angry and efficient toss, was so reminiscent of Dad, sober, absently piling up our toys in a garbage pyre in the center of a room.

"You just pitched her food, man," I said on more than one occasion.

"Did I?" he said. "Is it her food? Food doesn't belong to anyone. It belongs to the world. Feed the hungry."

"What, the fucking birds?"

"They need to eat, too," he said, before retreating downstairs, his back straight, his lats flexed.

Like I said, that was his kind of logic. And like I further said, I was glad when he was out of the house. I feel terrible saying that, but goddamn it, it's true.

"You should go see him," my wife repeated after opening night.

"I will," I promised. "Once the play's done." I shook my head. "The guy's Rasputin. I don't know how he survived."

"He has a strong constitution," Emily said, kissing me on the cheek. She had just showered and her hair glowed.

"I guess."

THANK GOD FOR THE PLAY. IT KEPT ME FOCUSED AND the cast and crew were very supportive—especially Denise as my wife who's trying to kill me because she wants a divorce (like I said, it's a comedy). Denise never did a line the same way twice. She brought energy to scenes and her choices helped inform mine.

And whenever I dropped a line she covered for me, whenever I started to wander from being in the moment—word to word, sentence to sentence—she helped bring me back, through a gesture, a look, or an inflected word. She has these huge eyes, supportive, understanding that asks you about you, that takes you seriously as you, that allows you to be yourself. I know I'm sounding vague on this, but she's one of those people who gives way more than she gets and I think I briefly fell in love with her because I needed something outside of all the confusions of the past. I don't know, but the theatre was the one thing I could count on. I didn't carry a cell phone, and I didn't have to worry about vodka and pills. And heroin.

Actors go on journeys, make discoveries, but the lines in a play are constant. If you're word perfect, the lines don't change, only your approaches do. There's security in that.

Anyway, one night after rehearsal my dad called.

"How's he doing?"

"I don't know, Dad."

My father hadn't seen my brother in years. Well, that's not completely true. Gary showed up at Babo's funeral (that's my dad's mom), said he was there to honor the past. "You hear me, Fat Man. I'm here to pay my respects," he said in a low challenging growl. Dad's second wife said Gary knew nothing about respect. "Where you been? You haven't seen your father in over eight years, you never call, and you come here and threaten, you threaten him. You're not a man, you're a midget."

Yeah, it sounds like a line out of a Samuel Fuller film—*Underworld USA*, maybe?—but that's what she said and Gary shut up. At least that's the story as told by my father. I wasn't there. I wouldn't really know.

"Well, tell him to take care. I love him."

"I'll tell him, Dad."

"You coming up this summer?"

"Yeah, when I'm done with the play."

ANOTHER IMAGE FROM CHILDHOOD. I MUST HAVE BEEN twelve, on the edge of puberty. My sister was eight. Gary, nine. Anyway, Mom was working at the boutique in the mall and Dad had taken us swimming and he never did that. We had a fun time at the pool, and he even splashed in the water, dunking us, laughing, spitting slivers in our faces. Everything was a bright glimmer. I should have known the mood couldn't last.

After three hours at the pool, we got home, and Dad made us all change in the doorway. I don't know why, but his eyes had a detached glint. We had to strip right there. He didn't want us to get the floors wet. He didn't even toss us any towels. Just take off your swimsuits, he said.

I don't think it was a sex thing. It was a control thing.

He wanted to break us.

You see, my family was never intimate. We weren't a huggy bunch. I think I saw my mother's left breast, once—I mean that's all. We didn't walk around nude or anything like that. Well, Dad did. He was uninhibited. Mom worried about the neighbors calling the police on him. She was always shutting curtains. The rest of us were pretty uptight.

So, we're begging Dad to not make us do this. Get us some towels to cover ourselves. Let Sis use the bathroom. It was right next to us, in the hallway, by the door. But he refused. He just stood there, arms crossed. I felt my heart in my shoulders and neck and chest. My brother bit his lower lip. Sis pulled off her bathing suit first. I remember it sticking to her thighs. And then she ran, I mean ran, upstairs.

"Pussies," Dad said to me and Gary.

And then we undressed too.

TOMORROW WE OPEN FOR THE FINAL WEEKEND. A local reviewer praised Denise. Said she worked on several emotional levels. She was funny, had dynamic range, and wonderfully expressive eyes. About me, I think the reviewer said something like "he's kind of an awkward cat, but funny, most of the time."

"Awkward"? "Funny"? I want to be serious.

Oh well, that's more or less the truth as I remember everything. As for my brother, he called me yesterday or maybe it was the day before.

He had just seen Iggy Pop and his revamped Stooges at Massey Hall. "Fucking awesome," he shouted into the phone. It must have been 2:30 in the morning and I live in the Central Time Zone. So it was 3:30 in T.O. "So when you coming up?"

"Next week. The kids are coming. Emily, too."

"I love your kids, man. And Emily, that goes without saying."

"Yeah."

"Fucking, Iggy, man. Fucking Iggy." The guy's like sixty Gary said, and he's still body surfing, laying it out there, man, diving into the crowd. My brother, drawn to Iggy's sweaty physicality, felt he was having a religious moment. "I know you go to church, man. I'm not being disrespectful."

"I know."

"Man. I had to touch him. I just had to." On the streetcar ride to the show, my brother cried all the way there. He didn't feel he deserved to see Iggy. He had lived a bad life. He had loved Susan but not enough and she died. But damn it the concert cost $119. So he forced himself out of the apartment. And once at the show, he felt reborn. "It was kind of like—I know you go to church, man—but—I had to touch him." So he worked his way through the sweat and the crowd of hands that were lifting, exalting Iggy. "I touched his lat, man. His fucking lat." It was like the Hosanna scene in the Bible.

"Cool."

"And he looked at me, you know, as if I were DeNiro in *Taxi Driver*. Like I'm some kind of nut, and then he smiled, like he knew I was okay."

"Well, you are."

"Yeah, I guess. He fucking smiled, man."

"Yeah." And I was smiling on the phone, listening to his joy, and I think he started crying again, I'm not sure, and I just wanted the moment of happiness and abandon to last, to last several days. Well one can hope several hours anyway, or at least until the damn morning. *Some* things have to be permanent, don't they?

And so we talked some more and in the silent spaces of our words I didn't see Iggy buoyed up by arms that looked like puffed palm leaves. Instead, Iggy crested above a sea of dead flowers, dry petals and stems drifting, as the singer was rising and falling, falling and rising.

Used and Abused

 ∿

H E SHOULD HAVE KNOWN THE NOTE WAS trouble as soon as he saw the ribbon of paper corkscrewed around a leg of his office desk. It wasn't even a full sheet, but the torn top eighth from a wide-ruled page. Above the jagged tear, in the white space, was written six words in small caps, the d's heavy with pregnant bottoms, the e's blocky with excessive weight. "Professor Steicher used and abused me," the note said.

Six words, six accusatory words, six words to report to the Department Head, but what did this note mean and who wrote it and why did they leave it with me, Associate Professor Lenny Meissner wondered.

He had just finished up his three-hour Tuesday night workshop. For twenty-five years, Professor Meissner taught creative writing at Hoover State College and edited *Middle American Review*. He had placed thirteen or so stories in quality magazines such as *Boulevard* and *Georgia Review*, but he didn't have a collection. His book on craft, *How to Put the Telling Back into Storytelling*, was published with Writer's Digest. Ten years ago the book stirred some interest, especially when Meissner quipped at an AWP roundtable session, "after all what we do isn't called storyshowing."

He opened his thermos and poured a last bitter cup of coffee. Perfect for the moment. Meissner's career was clearly eclipsed by Assistant Professor Curt Steicher, a creative writing colleague, a star. Two Pushcart Prizes, anthologized in Norton's *Fifteen Under Thirty-Five* collection, a Drue Heinz Prize collection of stories, and a novel forthcoming from Picador.

Steicher had been hired five years ago as the graduate program under Meissner grew. The first change the older professor noticed was fewer theses to direct as students opted for Steicher as chair. Meissner was fifty-five. Steicher, thirty-three, played in a local grunge band, and perhaps related to students better. His stories were often about characters drifting into random hookups and trying to extricate themselves from coercive relationships.

Meissner sipped coffee and stared at the note. It could be written by a man or a woman. The blocky letters with the ruler-edged bottoms resembled the work of an architectural design student. Curt had a wife, three girls with Old Testament names, and a two-story house on Main Street that was always brightly lit.

Meissner sighed heavily and wondered why he had to get caught in the possible undertow of this whole damn business. He didn't like Steicher much. Within a week or two of arriving in eastern Iowa, Steicher had dismissed Meissner as a has-been, never seeking his counsel or paying him any respect, and Meissner just as quickly sized up the junior colleague as a huckster.

Curt quickly brokered deals with other editors. After joining the editorial staff at *Middle American Review*, he entered into an "I'll publish yours if you'll publish mine" pact. In twenty years of editing Meissner avoided that. He even went so far as to pull his own stories from other magazines if, in the interim of waiting to hear from them, he had accepted a story by one of their editors for *Middle American*. Meissner was old-fashioned, regarded himself as a man of integrity, and that's probably why he had only a baker's dozen publications. To derail the Steicher Express, Meissner changed the policies at *Middle American Review*, granting himself final say on any and all stories tentatively accepted, effectively silencing in five years fifteen of Curt "Kid Pro Quo" Steicher's selections. It was a little mean-spirited but it had to be done.

Meissner sighed again, finished his coffee, and felt like his stomach was in his ankles.

Contrary to Meissner's personal dislikes, the students found Curt quite likable, but was he capable of what this note implied? Maybe. There was something twisted, controlling, and a bit sadistic to the man. At one party a year ago, Curt asked people to tell embarrassing stories. Confessions abounded from being sixteen and caught masturbating in the bathroom by your fourteen-year-old sister to accidently leaving a shirt unbuttoned and your bra exposed for a fifty-minute comp class. Curt's confession was a fizzle. When his turn came up, he smiled, and said he had never read *Moby-Dick*. That was it. *Moby-Dick*.

Meissner continued pondering—an affair, date rape? See the Department Head in the morning? Talk to the wife—she's usually got a good handle on these things. Don't confront Curt directly?

From his window the parking lot resembled a black shiny disc. There were no cars and a flagpole ping-pinged and wind rattled office glass. It was early March and cold. But not as cold as the mood in tonight's workshop. The stories weren't very strong. One lacked any kind of narrative arc. No character choices. A second felt like it was written while the student was text messaging. A third was three stories forced into one.

The worst aspect of it all was that Meissner had to play heavy—here's what's wrong, here's what's not working. He'll make suggestions but never collaborate—he won't rewrite stories for students. By contrast, Curt not only collaborates but encourages students to "steal from the best," which often includes himself. One of Curt's Pushcart Prize–winners ends with: "I talked and talked and talked." It was a bleak piece about the disconnect in a young couple, and the final repetitions suggested an inability to connect. It was quite good, Meissner had to admit. Apparently, one of Curt's star students, Susan Aaron Kerr, thought so too. Last month, she published a story in *Lone Star Review* that ended with the pithy line: "We talked and walked and talked and walked."

Professor Meissner was about to leave his office when he was startled by a gentle knock, like a riffle of wind chimes. It was Keith Apple, one of his better students. "Professor, can I see you for a minute?" he asked.

Everything Keith did was awkward, from the way he leaned his lanky frame and arms against a door as if he were hugging it to his comments in class that often veered from story proper to autobiographical anecdotes and how his connection to the personal made the story legit, real. But did Meissner really want to know that Keith sucked his thumb until he was twelve or didn't have sex until he was twenty-three? The professor invited him in.

Keith wore baggy jeans, a Hello Kitty T-shirt, black knit cap, and Buddy Holly glasses. He wanted to talk about his story, but Meissner suggested that he wait, give himself a cooling off period first, but Keith was insistent. His usual olive-hued face was raw and bright as if he had been sitting under a heat lamp.

"None of the chairs in your office match," he said, looking at the four variations.

"Uh-huh."

"Cool." He sat and opened his backpack. There were buttons all over it for various political candidates, rock bands, and left-wing causes. He pulled out all the responses and was agitated. Two students wrote nothing on his story; two didn't sign their comments, and one, an actor, wrote unjustified line edits everywhere. One four-sentence long paragraph had been converted by the student into six. "Now, they all sound the same. I deliberately thought about rhythm, here."

Meissner agreed and promised to say something to the class. This was art after all, so students shouldn't be too heavy-handed. If you're going to change a person's prose have a reason. Meissner then reiterated what he had said in workshop about Keith's story: it was over determined, the specimen character kept doing the same things in front of our peripheral narrator. Whenever things heated up, he had a meltdown and made a scene. Each moment replicated without adding to the previous ones. There was no narrative escalation.

"Yeah, I need more variation—"

"Is this a real uncle you're writing about? Forget that. Forget biography. Fictional rules are different from real-life rules, and this story is too real. Have your uncle act differently in the story. Give him dynamics."

"You said that in your book." He hunched forward, his hands on his knees. "The chapter on writing for the story first. Then the audience, then yourself."

"Yes, that's right."

"I love that book." He smiled, a tight sulky curl at the corner of his lips. His eyes were a dark chocolate brown.

"Well, look the comments over and then see me in a few days to talk some more. I thought this story was a step back from your previous one, but that's okay. You're trying things. Experimenting."

"How do you know which of your stories is good? I mean, I can see it in other people's work, like Susan's, but not my own, you know?"

Meissner nodded and rubbed his Hemingway style– beard. "I don't know. A click, I guess. I feel a click—"

"Wow, that's so mystical."

"Writing is."

Keith smiled and played with his knit cap, pushing it back before confessing that it had taken him weeks, since last semester, to find a story by Professor Meissner and he had finally tracked one down: a friend in California sent him a copy of *Palisades Review* featuring Meissner's "Hunters at the Laundromat." It was rich, Keith said, the characters authentic—nobody was perfect. The lead character made a mistake and tried to correct it as best he could. "How come you never share your work with us?"

"I don't want you to write like me."

"But, you can't help that. I mean, your chapter on telling, summary, and voice. That's pretty radical compared to the micro-detailing school. All of your students learn to do summary and that influences our style."

"Nothing you can't learn from John Cheever or Sherwood Anderson or Bernard Malamud—"

"Yeah, but—"

"It's just a different kind of detailing," Meissner said. "It's still your vision I'm nurturing."

"You ever notice in Steicher's stories there's no smells, nothing—"

"I didn't notice."

"The guy has no nose—"

Meissner told Keith that he didn't want to run down a faculty member and the young student apologized, looked up from his knees, and suggested that Professor Meissner should give a reading. He and Susan, president of the Student Association of Graduates in English, thought it was long overdue. "Your work is great."

"How is Susan?" She hadn't said much in class tonight. One comment per story—usually at the beginning of each critique.

Keith shrugged slowly. "Not so good. She thought the stories were shit. Mine included." He laughed.

Susan's last story was about failed relationships and delayed reunions. It was a quiet first-person piece that ended with pumpkin seeds tossed in a backyard and the character waiting to see what might happen next. Meissner encouraged her to send it out.

"Her stuff is so subtle you know—quiet, muted," Keith said. "I'm always over the top, like a standup comic loose on the page. 'Hello, nice lady,'" he said.

"That's a good Jerry Lewis," Meissner laughed, and then surprised Keith by saying, "I'll do a reading for SAGE."

"Really?"

"Yes." Meissner also surprised himself.

"Awesome." Keith gathered up his stories and returned them to his backpack. Seven he left on the table. There weren't any comments there worth keeping, including those from the actor and his damn line edits.

Don't be too harsh, Meissner said, there could be one jewel of wisdom there.

"Well, that's just it, I don't like jewelry," Keith said.

"So, is there anything else you wanted to talk to me about?" Meissner wondered if this impromptu gathering had anything to do with the note corkscrewed under his door, but he didn't want to overplay the scene.

"Yes." Keith looked away and said he had heard rumors about Curt getting drunk at receptions for visiting writers and hooking up with various students.

"Where did you hear this?"

"Well." He crossed one long, thin leg over a knee. "I've seen it, myself." He folded his arms across his chest. "I think that's why Susan's upset."

"She's seen it too?"

"No." He dropped his leg and leaned forward, his shoulders rising. "She was a victim."

Professor Meissner's stomach returned to his ankles.

He held up a hand and then rubbed his beard. Before they went any further with this conversation Keith had to know that Meissner would now have to report this to the Department Head and the Office of Compliance and Equity. Keith said that was fine.

A couple of weeks ago, during Larry Watson's reading, there was a party and Curt slept with Susan Aaron Kerr. Afterward, he told her he could no longer direct her thesis.

"That's all he said?"

"Yes. And—" He shrugged. "She's been upset about it ever since." Moreover, Susan had also shown the story about the pumpkin seeds, the one Meissner workshopped two weeks ago, to Curt and he thought it was thin. The language didn't sing and the characters were shallow. He was tired with reading about girls who were less interested in boys and more interested in friendships with their older brothers.

"I think it's publishable," Meissner huffed. He showed Keith the note that he found under the door, asked if it was Susan's handwriting, and then regretted sharing it with a student.

"I'm not sure."

"And I'm not sure what to do next," Meissner added.

THE NEXT DAY, MEISSNER MET DEPARTMENT CHAIR Tony Staios in his office. Staios looked at the crinkled paper as if it were radioactive, said the perpetrator of these rumors and innuendo hadn't even signed it, and as department head he was not recommending that anything else be done further up the line until there was more evidence. "Just drop it," he said. Besides, he reminded Lenny, Curt was one of the most liked members of our faculty and had recently won a University-wide undergrad teaching award. "Who knows who wrote this damn thing. It's gutless."

Meissner couldn't agree with that—it seemed more like a cry for help, and he couldn't drop it. He tried. After meeting with Tony, Meissner read some stories in his office but kept thinking about the note, the desperation behind it—perhaps it was the chivalric streak in him and his desire to protect and defend women, but he had to do something. Last night, Lenny didn't even discuss the note with his wife because he found the whole subject too messy.

Now Meissner walked the lean, dim-lit hallways, hands in pockets, left curling about the ribboned note. If Curt had slept with Susan, he did it during a semester in which she wasn't one of his students so he hadn't broken any protocols. Secondly, by removing himself from her thesis, he saved himself from being open to any additional attacks from the English Department or the Dean or the Provost's office. But, if what had transpired with Susan was something less than consensual then Curt was in big trouble.

Curt's office door was open and he was gently railing against a student's particular brand of minimalism, saying it wasn't working. "It's like you need a big hand right here, pointing at these words, saying, 'hey, this here's important, dear reader.' You follow?" "Yes." The fatigue in the student's voice embarrassed Meissner. "I like the grit though and the milieu," Curt said. "But the characters are a little shallow."

"How shallow?"

"Oh, I don't know. Let's just say shallow enough to drown in the story's water."

The student said nothing and Meissner poked his head in and wondered if he and Curt could talk as soon as the student left.

Curt, wearing a gray sweater and Buster Browns, smiled, said sure, but it had to be quick. He was off to play racquetball with a member of the Philosophy and Religion Department. Meissner gave an absent-minded wave and waited in the hall. Curt didn't respect Meissner, the older professor suspected, because Kid Pro Quo had an MFA and Meissner had only an MA with a creative writing emphasis.

Whatever the reason, the two never really got along and rarely served on theses directed by the other. Meissner sighed. It had already been a slow morning. For *Middle American Review* he had found a decent story about a woman going to AA, but the ending, an echo of an earlier line, was too heavy of an echo, a bad rhyme. So he wrote some nice words on the rejection slip and encouraged the writer to submit again. Curt's signs of encouragement were too much. He always touched female students: at receptions, he placed a hand on the small of a back; at bars after a reading, he patted a forearm; and when Susan got her first story published, Curt hugged her in the hall outside the main office. It was a sideways hug, but—

Five, ten minutes passed, and Curt peeked his head around the doorframe. He apologized and said, "I hear you're giving a reading." The freckles on his face seemed to be moving, vibrating like little atoms.

"Yes." News travels. Meissner nodded and followed Curt into his office. A portrait of Franz Kafka and Curt's Utah PhD, framed in black, hovered above his desk, and several signed baseballs were in little glass cubes along a bookshelf. "So what's going on with Susan?" On the opposite wall hung a drumhead from a kick. It was of the New York Dolls and featured sprawled autographs scratching across the band logo and an illustration of a young woman bending over, a skirt riding up her thighs. It was as if Curt were still an undergrad.

"Susan?" Curt sat back in an office chair that shifted with his weight. His hands were behind his head, leather patches under elbows.

"New York Dolls?"

"Jerry Nolan, a great drummer."

Meissner remained standing and nodded and wondered how appropriate that kick head was—expensive relic or not—for female students to be greeted by. Curt's grunge band, 76 Trombones and a Hand Grenade, played once a month at local bars. The band's lead guitarist was a grad student of Curt's. "Susan dropped you as thesis chair?"

"Yeah, well," Curt shrugged. "You know how that is." The chair clanked as he leaned forward. His last few comments on her stories were too harsh for her and she felt that he was controlling her artistic vision, not giving her the space she wanted. "Differences of opinion. I think she can be really good, but she's not willing to push herself enough. And she resents my pushing her."

"I thought her last story was brilliant."

"Really? Nothing happened."

"Yes, it did. She, Tara, the character, is taking small, baby steps. It's not a full change but a quasi-change. She'll track down her brother eventually. Just not right now."

"I thought it was weak. I mean what's with the pumpkin seeds?"

"It's an anti-epiphany story."

"Oh, don't give me that Charles Baxter 'Against Epiphanies' shit. The story was too quiet."

Maybe Curt told Susan the same thing he said to this morning's student—put a big hand here with a finger pointing, telling us to pay attention, Dear Reader. "Anything happen between you two?"

"What do you mean?"

"Well, you're not even a reader for the thesis." Meissner had checked with Deanna the department secretary earlier in the morning.

"No, clean break. That's how she wanted it." He tightened his arms across his chest. "You know, I think I should create a T-shirt for AWP that says 'Just Because You're Misunderstood Doesn't Make You a Genius.' That's Susan. She's good, but she can't take criticism. She's so hard done by." He rolled his eyes dramatically. "Every little bit of criticism she gets all intense about. And she's no genius."

Meissner didn't know what to say, and then said that this was awkward, but what the hell, sorry, and showed Curt the ribboned note. Curt's face whitened and his freckles tightened. He rubbed his small chin and smiled a lopsided grin, his upper lip trembling. "What the fuck's this?" he said.

Found it last night under the office door, Meissner said.

"It doesn't mention Susan here—"

"I know, but I heard from Keith Apple—"

"That talentless hack—that guy's a nut—"

"He's not a nut—he's—eccentric, awkward—" In two semesters, Keith's writing had really taken off. He started off with sound effects in his stories and all caps when people yelled and five exclamation marks at the end of excited phrasings. His first story opened with an alarm clock ringing. Now he was writing low-key, working-class, character-driven material and he had just sent out two stories, one to *Glimmer Train* and the other to the *MacGuffin*.

"You two were talking about me behind my back—?"

"He talked to me about Susan."

"Fucking nut job."

"Look, I haven't reported this to anyone." Well he had, but Tony was dropping it, so it was like Lenny had said nothing. "If it's not Susan who wrote the note, then there's someone else. There's a problem here—"

"I don't see a problem. I see innuendo. I see false accusations." He pushed off from his chair, and it swayed and clattered behind him. "I did not use and abuse anyone. This conversation's done." He crushed the note in his right hand.

"Look, I need the note back."

"Hell, no. This is my rep we're talking about. No—"

"That's—" He wanted to say "evidence" but stopped himself.

"Talk to Susan, ask her, see what she has to say." He tore the ribbon into tiny fragments and flecked them into a wastebasket. One or two pieces fell to the floor like spots of lint. "I dare you to find hard evidence against me." Now he sounded like Michael Corleone before the Senate's investigative committee on organized crime.

"I'll talk to Susan," Lenny said softly.

"Fine," he said. "That's just fine."

Maybe above his desk Curt should also hang a portrait of Hemingway to rub elbows with Kafka. Fine, indeed.

A FEW DAYS LATER UNDER THE PRETENSE OF DISCUSSING one of her stories that he wanted to publish in *Middle American*, Professor Meissner met up with Susan Aaron Kerr at a coffee shop on Main Street next to a community theatre. He told her that once she finished her thesis the story would appear. In the meantime, Meissner didn't want there to be any competitive jealousies with her fellow grad students and asked her to keep mum about the upcoming pub.

She agreed, saying that Curt often got into trouble with charges of favoritism involving the guitarist in his band. "Shit, his stories suck, but Curt defends them in workshops. In one nothing happened. A bunch of guys went out and got drunk and almost drove a car into a lake."

Meissner smiled, thinking about pumpkin seeds, and studied the thin angular crease between Susan's eyebrows. It darkened, as she got agitated. When she wasn't irritated, her gray eyes were full of mischief. Susan was an iconoclast who often caught Meissner off guard by saying unexpectedly cynical and trenchant truths. He enjoyed that about her.

He also liked meeting at a coffee shop because whatever they said didn't have to be reported to the Department Head or the Office of Compliance and Equity. But so far not much had been said, and Meissner was distracted by Susan's mocha with a volcano of cream and a cherry on top. Was coffee ever served with cherries? Meissner went with the more straightforward red eye, no sugar, and no cream. He felt a little embarrassed by his selection because it ran counter to the real reason for his visit, which was anything but straightforward.

"I'm so excited about the story—it took me three semesters to get it right—"

Meissner nodded, sipping his red eye, wondering if there was any subtext in the forthcoming short story. Was there anything in it drawn from her relationship with Steicher? In the story, a girl feels abandoned by her big brother, discovers he lives in a small town, moves there and works at the post office in the hopes that her brother will see her behind the counter some day. But the random encounter doesn't occur and she takes out her frustrations by painting murals—in the park, under bridges, deep in sewer tunnels. Her boyfriend insists that she sign the murals but Tara never does. One Halloween he carves up pumpkins, stealing images from her murals. Then they accidently burn the seeds and Tara tosses them in the backyard, hoping for something new to grow. It was a subtle objective correlative and quite moving. "I was wondering about the boyfriend, in the story?" He seemed a bit underdeveloped.

"He's just a fun guy, you know? Makes her feel like having fun. He isn't really her boyfriend." She gestured with a small hand. Susan's hands didn't fit her full figure or energy—they were too contained. Meissner smiled, trying to follow the movements of her hands instead of the curves of her ample chest.

Those curves filled out a caramel red sweater that Meissner recalled seeing her in at a reading last semester. Susan often arrived late to readings. Just before the reader took the microphone, there she'd invariably be, and Curt would unfold a metal chair and set it in the front row. Hands church-like in her lap, Susan nodded rhythmically to the writer's key turns of phrase and character reversals. At one party, Susan paired off with an African American Pen/Faulkner winner from New Jersey who said that all he ever needed to learn about point of view he got from Raymond Chandler. Meissner preferred Dick Francis.

"He's not that important to the story," she said, her chest nudging the edge of the Formica table. "I mean they've slept together maybe three or four times—fuck buddies, that's all."

"Fuck buddies?"

Susan's eyes brightened. "You are so square, Professor."

"That's me."

A fuck buddy was "a friend who occasionally slept with you with no strings."

"But," Meissner tapped the top of his coffee cup. "What if one of the two thought there was more to it than that?"

"Then—" she said, studying the Monet-style paintings hanging across the way, "there'd be an inequality and a permeating sadness."

"Right." Her white blond hair touched the tops of her shoulders—the hair along the part was slightly darker than what tapped her cheeks like quote marks. Susan, twenty-six, twenty-seven, had taken three years off between degrees to work at a homeless shelter in the Twin Cities. Meissner tried drumming up other fast facts to avoid her beauty. "I don't think I've experienced that," Meissner said. "The unrequited thing."

"I have." She returned her gaze to the Impressionist likeness of Monet.

At twenty-one, Susan had a play she wrote produced by her small liberal arts college. At twenty-two she quit playing the trombone because a boyfriend didn't like the sound. Facts. What were the facts with regard to Steicher, the real story? Meissner felt awkward. How obligated was the older professor to truth or was he after something else, a desire to destroy a younger man whose art was truly great but whose private life left a lot to be revised. If only writers could rewrite, revise, their personal lives instead of the manuscripts they cherished and sent forth into the world. Curt's character needed to be overhauled—the fault was in his character. Touching women at parties and receptions, hugging in the hallways past the point of comfort, and praising their fiction. It was the men in workshops who suffered Steicher's heated attacks, as he had to diminish them all. At least, that's what Keith Apple told Meissner, and two or three other disgruntled male students had come forward yesterday, including one who last semester petitioned to have his status in the class switched to pass/fail. Now, Meissner's eyes stung as if they were sensitive to light. "That unrequited thing—with Curt?" The room suddenly felt like it was warping.

"How did you know?" She hunched forward in her chair, crowding the table's edge, her eyes dampening.

He had heard about it not just from Keith but two other male students corralled this morning for information. "Did you leave a note under my door?"

"Note?"

"I don't—Curt tore it up." He repeated the note's six words and how he might have to report this unless he can clear it up, and then she glanced at her drink, the cream, a sinking iceberg. "Used and abused" was something she had said. She realized it was clichéd as soon as she said it, then and now, but she repeated the mantra that night, drunk at a party—she couldn't help herself. "Isn't that what we do when we're upset, talk in clichés?"

But the words she didn't mean, she was just saying them, being melodramatic, a creative-writing diva. She had slept with Curt, twice—

"I don't need—details—"

"But you *do* need to know. Professor Steicher could be in trouble—"

"Yes—that's true—I'm not—I'm just trying to—"

"We slept together. It was consensual. I was hurt. I said some things. They weren't true."

"But you didn't leave me a note?"

"No." Her eyes studied the dissipating cream. "No."

She wanted more than being a fuck buddy.

"And that's when you dropped him from your thesis?"

"He did. University rules." There was a catch to her voice. "He can't chair my shit once he's slept with me."

"Well, it's not the sixties anymore." Meissner apologized as soon as he said it.

She looked cross. "You are a square."

"Yes, I am. But I'm a good teacher, and I'll help make your fiction better."

A dim gleam returned to her eyes and she half-smiled. Curt had also slept with one of his former undergrad advisees, a non-trad twenty-four-year-old with a Native American name like Lakota Autumn or something, but she's white, Susan said.

"Sounds like an Indian name in a bad Western."

"He dropped her too once he slept with her. He's not breaking any rules."

"Then who wrote the damn note? There's someone out there who does feel like they need to talk about it. Who feels exploited?"

"Exploited?" She laughed. "I had a good time and he's pretty good."

"I don't need to hear about it."

"He's good—I'll tell you that." And she'd been with a few of those two-hump chump types—nice respectable boys with money. Usually from Des Moines.

"I wish you wouldn't." Meissner coughed up some of his red-eye. "You like shocking me, don't you?"

"Yeah. You're such a prude." She stirred her coffee. "It was consensual. Can we talk now about my damn story?"

"Yes, I'm convinced after what you said about, you know, fuck buddies, that there's no changes needed. Just probably some minor stuff I'll AQ later."

She tilted her head left while nodding. "Used and Abused. Used and Abused." The only person she repeated those words to was Keith. At a party, she was in a funk and then fell into Joan Crawford land. Keith rubbed her back, followed her, sequestered pretzels, brought her cold drinks—beer, then water—and probably wanted to sleep with her, she said, but she wasn't interested. "Anyway, I like him—but—he's a little weird." She paused. "He heard me prattle about Curt and my feelings. You don't suppose—?"

"Fuck," Meissner said, as pain gathered like dark clouds behind his eyes.

KEITH APPLE ADMITTED THE WHOLE THING EARLY THE next morning in Professor Meissner's office. He said he didn't like how Steicher used and abused women—Apple counted four in the last two years—and if nobody was going to do a damn thing about it, hell, he was.

"Who appointed you judge, Keith?"

His double blue flannel ensemble, black jeans, and spotless white tennis shoes looked more casual than the moment warranted. "Somebody had to," he said, his voice thin, almost a faint shrug.

The truth was you wanted Susan for yourself, Meissner said, feeling strangely like a detective in a Bogart movie. And when she wouldn't hook up with you, you wanted to get even with *both* of them.

"Never with Susan. I wasn't trying to hurt her—"

"You implicated her. And didn't you think of what she might say if I talked to her?" Revelations about a certain beer-drinking party pointed the finger, the big hand in Steicher's margins, right at Keith Apple. Look here, dear reader.

Keith removed his Buddy Holly glasses and wiped tired eyes. Dent marks, Frankenstein feet, were at the sides of his nose. "I guess I didn't." He now chewed down on a triangle collar to one of his two flannel shirts. "But I wasn't trying to get even—"

"And why did you drag me into this mess?" Meissner couldn't control the irritated edge cutting through his voice.

Keith toyed with the zipper of his backpack, apologized feebly, his lower lip parted, the sulky curl returning to the corners of his mouth. Meissner was the better teacher, Keith said, and it was a raw deal how so many grad students wanted to work with Steicher as their Chair. Shit, just because he won a Pushcart Prize. "Two," Meissner corrected. Whatever, Steicher coddled favorites like that Johnny Thunders wannabe in his band, passed judgment at the end of each workshop on whether or not the story up for discussion was publishable, made deals with other editors to promote himself, and encouraged students to write like him. "He never liked my work." Steicher was anti-minimalism, and Keith was a minimalist.

The clouds of hurt now pounded behind Meissner's eyes. Within days following Professor Meissner's report to the Department Head, Dean of the College, and

Provost, Keith Apple would be removed from classes at Hoover State College and sent to Iowa City for psychiatric evaluation. He wouldn't return to the college, but would eventually finish his degree at Iowa State and sell electronics at Best Buy before entering local politics in Ames.

But in that confessional moment between playing with the zipper on his backpack and looking around at four unmatched chairs in the office, in that instant between Apple's castigating gaze at Steicher and the pain returning to Meissner's eyes, the senior professor sadly heard echoes of his own in the young student's words. Chivalry and human rights were never the issue; a need to fathom into the deep recesses of another man's desires in order to find evidence against him was. And for this the professor was truly ashamed.

AFTER MEETING WITH KEITH APPLE, MEISSNER couldn't find Curt in his office, nor the main office, and his colleague didn't attend the afternoon department meeting.

There, Tony Staios pushed ahead the provost's plan to lower the ACT exemption for comp to 25, effectively reducing the size of classes and demand for adjuncts. Lenny grumbled in the corner and said that was really dumb—"you can't put a number on writing proficiency."

"Twenty per cent budget cuts. We've got no choice," Staios said.

Following the meeting, Meissner visited Curt's two-story house on Main.

It was late afternoon, the sun a poached egg above

the horizon line, and Curt's house was as brightly lit as always. All of the angular windows shone and even the hexagonal-shaped porch light was on. Wind chimes sparkled and behind the house droned the occasional nasal mutterings of ducks.

Mary, Curt's wife, opened the door, a slight smile at the corners of her mouth. She said a quick hello, and seemed a bit embarrassed about her lack of formal attire: she had just got home from her position as a secretary in the foundation office and changed into gray sweats. Her blond-streaked hair was wrapped in a bandana and she smelled of perfume and okra. "Stew?" Meissner asked. "Is it supper time? I can leave."

"No, no." Dinner was another forty-five minutes away. She invited him in, and he told her how great it smelled. "Beef. Carrots. Potatoes. Okra, right? With— curry powder and cumin?"

"Yes," she said.

One of Curt's girls watched TV in the living room— it was a Disney sitcom with a bad laugh track. Another daughter, curled up in a wet-looking leather chair, read a *Twilight* series book. A third, eleven-year-old Leah, whom Meissner recognized, slapped a mini-soccer ball against a baseboard. Left, right, laterally she roamed, but the ball thudded to a consistent, accurate kicking rhythm against a worn spot.

Mary called upstairs for Curt, referring to Professor Meissner as Leonard. Only his wife called him that, but Mary charmed him. She had no pretenses and it was obvious from the slight, painful smile that she knew of Curt's infidelities and handled them without drama. She was one of those curvy Scandinavian women that populate Iowa, filled with a stillness that Meissner admired: strong, reserved, and subtle. He smiled politely and realized he was writing her as a character for a future story. He often did that—romanticized women, and that's clearly what got him into trouble with that covert note. Chivalry and professional jealousies guided his responses. Mary placed a hand to the side of her neck. "Curt's upstairs. Writing." Meissner nodded as she excused herself to the kitchen.

Leah hadn't missed the spot on the baseboard yet, the dull thudding filling the house with urgency, and Curt arrived, all three buttons of his Polo shirt undone. "Today's my writing day."

"Sorry. I didn't mean to interrupt—"

"That's fine I was just finishing up a key scene." He loved how fiction took him places he didn't expect to go. "A character is taking over the moment—it's awesome."

Along the dining room's far wall was a bench, cubbyholes full of large Fisher-Price toys, dolls with stringy hair, and scraps of board games. Meissner wished he had been as confident early in his career as Curt. Lenny would never dare to miss a department meeting. But for Curt, tenure was a lock. Two fishing rods were also on the bench.

Curt dropped his hands to his hips. "Dinner's still a half hour away. What's up?"

Lenny absently walked to the bench and hefted one of the rods. He hadn't fished since he was a kid. The rod felt light and alive in his hands. "Never had the patience for this—"

Curt smiled. The kids liked fishing in the creek behind the house. "It's not that deep. Catfish mainly."

Leah's taps were lighter now, the ball arcing off the
baseboard at a shorter distance. "I just wanted you to
know that the charges against you were totally unfound-
ed." Without going into too much detail, Meissner said
the letter or note was a put-up job by a misguided, jealous student.

"The nut, Buddy Holly?"

"Yes. Keith."

"The guy's a tool." Curt shook his head, and then
directed Lenny through the kitchen and on out to his
backyard patio. A barbecue was off to the side, foil drip-
ping out of its closed lid. Angular trees swayed gently
in the breeze, the tops of their branches darker than the
rest of the bark. From the creek rose a quiet, adenoidal
muttering.

"Mallards," Curt said catching the expression on
Lenny's face. "There's a husband and wife that we've
been seeing for three years on their way to wherever
they visit." He shrugged and the adenoidal blur was now
chattering.

Lenny squinted in the sun's glare. It was no longer
cold but he placed his hands in his pockets. "I'm sorry
for causing you stress."

Curt laughed with anger and raised an abrupt hand.
He kicked at wedged stones dotting the patio's concrete
edgings. To Lenny, it was like watching his own son,
summers ago at six, smacking his hand into his mitt and
worrying stones on the infield. "'Stress.' That's funny. I
think my BP's off the charts." He turned away from the

sun and walked a step or two toward the barbecue. With his back turned, he mentioned that he had an "open" marriage. His wife wasn't happy with his "dalliances," but he never kept anything from her.

"Oh."

The ducks' chatter suggested distant Tommy guns.

Curt turned, hands pressed against his thighs, lips thinly parted. "You know in your book, that chapter of yours, 'Why Read Chekhov,' you spoke eloquently about the writer's even-handed tone." Often, Curt assigned that chapter in his creative writing classes and promoted Meissner's call for nonjudgment. "What is it you said, Lenny? 'Don't judge your characters. Live in them, be them'—I think that's what you said."

"Uh-huh, that's it."

Curt paused, his blue eyes narrowing, freckles seemingly vibrating with the sun's glare. "And yet, and yet, when it came to me you didn't treat me the same way."

There was no answer for that, Meissner said. No real answer. The ducks' Tommy gun chatters spit in the silences. "I—I—"

"I suppose Tony pushed ahead that damn ACT exemption?"

"Yes. Twenty-five. We'll lose a fourth of our comp students and several adjunct faculty."

"I swear this college has become open-line dependent. We skirt education to save money. Students need writing classes."

Lenny agreed with Curt and the chattering ducks had progressed to a competitive squawking. "So, writing a new novel?"

"No. Well, maybe. I don't know. I don't know what it is yet. Could be nonfiction. There's a lot of my father in the story. He was an alcoholic."

"So was mine."

Curt smiled. He shrugged with fatigue.

"If you need a reader—?"

Just then the back door banged open and closed as Curt's kids, responding to the ducks' rising chatter ran from the house, tunnels of white bread tucked against their thin arms. Leah still dribbled a mini-soccer ball. One of the other daughters, Hannah or Rebecca, handed Professor Meissner two pieces of bread. "For the ducks," she said.

The ground was soft, the grass—in spots—brown, and Meissner tried not to think of the mud staining his shoes as he followed the Steichers to the creek's edge and those noisy ducks. They hurried down a bare path, over broken branches and leafy remains, and once the ducks saw them, Lenny and the Steichers were surrounded as chattering funneled and cycloned about. Postage stamps of bread fell, and Mary told one of the girls to be careful, your fingers, and the Steicher daughters laughed, and the ducks kicked up more adenoidal fuss. As Meissner's smiles of appreciation spread, the bits of bread, the nasal mutterings, and the ducks and their circular commotion were just as quickly gone.

Faraway Girl

❧

O VER THE YEARS, THE THING THAT JIM NOTICED about her more than anything else was the eyes, a faraway look that suggested contentment and concern, a confusion with the world. Melissa Coors was an odd girl. Some said she was slow, but Jim never thought of her that way—he preferred childlike over "mildly retarded." Melissa had a long attention span for things that interested her—like the Sunday morning funnies, Fats Waller records, and afternoon ballgames at the Polo Grounds.

He knew her ever since they were kids, sweeping the floors and polishing the chrome of his father's saloon. When Melissa was but thirteen and Jim fifteen, he rescued her from a shag shack. Jim had heard about it from Grace Simek, a childhood friend, and when he found Melissa wearing only a man's striped pajama top in a room dimly lit with kerosene lamps, he shoved the boys aside, told them to collect their money and get. One sulky lad objected, and Jim broke his nose on two punches. On their walk home, Melissa wondered if she could get ice cream.

She rarely understood the consequences of her choices. For her there was nothing wrong in experimenting with these boys, and Jim didn't want to patronize her with a lecture, but he suggested how a wingless bird could never get off the ground. "Well doing this with those boys is like being wingless, you understand?" She agreed, tilting her head right, as a teardrop of ice cream kissed her chin.

Offbeat metaphors aren't something that a slow, "retarded" kid understands. Melissa did. After the Great War, Jim saw Melissa occasionally, whenever he was back in New York to visit family over a holiday or to promote his latest film. Last Christmas he brought her some fashion pictures used as a tie-in for *Public Enemy*. Melissa thought the photographs of Jim in a double-breasted Brooks Brothers were a bit too dull—"the world should be full of color"—so she finger-painted over each image with green and orange.

Jim, following a long cab ride, now sat in front of Melissa's father in the Coors's three-room flat in Yorkville, Jim's childhood haunt. He felt guilty: glad to no longer live in this neighborhood and relieved to get his mind off his Hollywood troubles. Melissa was missing and he now had something to do. When Jim walked off the Warner Brothers lot to protest low wages, typecasting, and his onscreen roughhousing of women, the thirty-two-year-old actor had no idea that his exile to a Greenwich Village apartment with wife Billie could last this long (four months) or that it would possibly lead to this new adventure. Mr. Johnson Coors, a family friend and a former regular at Pop's saloon up until Pop died from the 1919 Pandemic, gave the "retired" actor a recent photograph of Melissa, taken out front of a drugstore.

Missy was "borderline, you know?" Johnson said, lighting a cigarette. His fingers were short, stubby, and yellow. His left eye was higher on his face than his right.

Missy, in the photo, stared dully into the sun, eyes creased. She was now pushing thirty, but still looked like a girl. Her breasts were small, shoulders angular, and her face lacked guile. The look of her eyes reminded Jim a bit of himself. Whenever he ruminated too much or slipped into a blue mood over poverty, injustice, or his own acting career, others would call him the "faraway fella."

Jim rubbed at the edge of his lips. The Coors' apartment was a wet washcloth that needed to be wrung out. "Like I promised on the phone, I'll be glad to help, Mr. Coors."

"Don't call me Mister, Jimmy. You're too old for that. Johnson's fine."

"No problem," Jim grinned. Across from him was a glass of orange juice that looked like it had been poured last week. Hardened food was stuck to plates stacked by the kitchen sink. A handle on the icebox was loose.

"I loved when you killed that horse," Johnson said.

Jim nodded.

Johnson opened a bag of potato chips and dumped them into a bright bowl. He pushed it between them. "Is it true for the grapefruit scene the original script called for an omelet?"

It was. "Let's not talk about that—tell me about Melissa."

Shards of chips fell from Johnson's lips and left little slits of stains on his white shirt. "We're just so proud of you, Jimmy, my boy. Local boy makes good."

Jim hated being called Jimmy—a Warner Brothers locution—he preferred Jim or James, his father's name. He reached for the chips and thought better of it—he had put on five pounds since going on strike.

Johnson's story: three weeks ago, Melissa had run off with Moishe Kupperberg, former pitcher of the Yorkville Nut Club. Jim played for the club from 1918-22 and caught all of Moishe's games. That tall, lanky lefthander had a wicked fade-away that came in on right-handers and cut the plate at their knees.

Moishe was a talker, a kibitzer with a big personality that could be so charming and elusive at the same time. When Jim caught Moishe's games, it was hard picking up the ball, because Moishe's release point was never the same—overhand, three-quarters, side. And his wonky motion, in a shirt that was three sizes too big, was full of deception and random subterfuge, arms and angular elbows flapping like broken off chicken wings. The ball, lost in this camouflage of loose-fitting movement, left batters and Jim wondering, *What am I not seeing?*

Now a lawyer, Moishe worked in a mid-town office, Dwann and Associates, but recently quit and his whereabouts and those of Missy were unknown. "Surely, he had to join a new office somewhere." Johnson took a slow drag from his cigarette. He was afraid that Melissa had become Moishe's sex slave.

Jim couldn't figure on that one. Moishe was a homosexual.

"What does she really know about making love?" Johnson's eyes narrowed like Missy's in the photograph and he shoved hair behind an ear. "And why else would

Moishe be interested in her? She's functioning at a nine-year-old level." He grabbed another handful of chips.

She was much smarter than nine. "Are they still in New York?"

"I think so." Missy had called a few nights ago and talked to her dad for twenty-five minutes. "If she were out of town the conversation would have been a lot shorter."

Jim agreed and drummed his fingers along the top of the kitchen table. "Okay." He'd start with the law office and see what he could find. They'd probably have a forwarding address.

Maybe Moishe needed a "cover" to protect his professional life and image. Years ago, during a long rain delay, Moishe made a pass at Jim and upon being turned down apologized profusely for being "such a degenerate."

So what did he want with the girl?

"I'm sorry it's so messy in here," Johnson said, "but I haven't got Missy to help me."

"Yeah."

"You sure you don't want any chips?"

"No, I'm good," Jim said. "I'm good."

LATE THE NEXT MORNING JIM WAS STANDING IN ONE OF the paneled offices of Dwann and Associates. Moishe was across from him. The lawyer was only in his early thirties, but with his fading hair and razor-thin mustache he looked over forty. Jim was puzzled to find him. He had been led to believe that Moishe had run off with Melissa—life was nothing like a Hollywood movie.

"What, no. I had left the office for a few days that's all. A honeymoon." He parked his hands on his hips, threw back his head, and released a short burst of laughter. "Platonic. She wanted to go see Niagara Falls and so we did." They even stole a pillow from the motel—"how corny can you get, huh?"

"That's a lot of corn—"

"I don't know why her father's dragging you into this. The girl's over 21."

"That's a technicality from her dad's point of view."

"She's not as dumb as everyone says. A little dim, but not dumb." He shuffled the fanned folders across his desk, hit the intercom button, and asked his secretary to hold all calls for the next fifteen minutes.

The day of the shag shack, Melissa was naive and desperate for love. Not much had changed for her over the years—she still looked like a child, but Moishe, a slum kid like Jim who also hung out front of saloons, had made the big-time: a private secretary in an adjoining office, a Dictaphone, and long angular windows that overlooked Manhattan.

"So, uh, yeah. The girl's with me." Moishe held up a sharp hand, moved to the door and closed it. "That's where she wants to be, Jimmy."

Jim nodded.

"Hell, Jimmy, it's great to see you. So tell me, you ever, you know, with Joan Blondell?"

"What? No, she's a friend—I'm married—"

"So?" He held out his hands as if to say don't kid a kidder. "With an ass like that."

"Moishe, please. Don't be a schmuck."

137

"I go by Moses here. It's a goy office, you know, gotta fit in." He shrugged.

"*Azoy vert dus kuchel tzekrokhen.*" Jim looked at the carpet—it had bird patterns in the weave. On the office desk, teetering at the edge of a blotter, was a tin toy monkey with cymbals.

"You crazy Irish Mick. You're a better Yid than me." He laughed. "Anyway, *Blonde Crazy*. Great movie. Funny. You should do more comedy. You crack me up. Like when you killed the horse in—"

"Everybody loved when I killed the horse. Look, Moses, enough kibitzing, I'm here about Melissa."

"Jim. I'm not, you know, with Melissa. We're friends. I'm a cake eater. Was a cake eater—it's complicated." Moses reminded Jim of how good-natured he had been over the rain-delay pass. Most fellas would've belted me, "but you just softly said no."

"I'm just a quiet kind of a fella, I guess." Jim absently flexed fingers and curled them into a fist.

"Not on screen. Man, that horse." Moishe laughed again. "Look, come to dinner tonight, see Melissa, and you'll see how happy she is. We'll talk all about it."

"Why don't we talk a little bit now, huh? You told the secretary fifteen minutes." Jim looked at his watch. "It's only been three." He grinned. *I don't get it—I mean, why her? What are you getting out of this?*

Moishe reached for a cigarette and offered Jim one. "Haven't picked up the habit? I thought everyone in Hollywood—"

Jim hadn't picked up on a lot of things in Tinseltown, and one of them was to be deferential to the bosses. Earlier that morning, Jim had received a telegram from Warners reminding him that he couldn't do any stage work while he was "on leave" in New York—and that Frank Capra, on behalf of the motion picture Academy, might get involved in negotiations. The studio also took the liberty to pitch him their next film, something about two-fisted cab drivers. "Great," Jim said to his Bill. "That's a real stretch from the work I've been doing."

Billie patted him on the side and kissed him. She smelled of strawberries and cigarettes. "It's okay. You'll find a way to make it your own."

"Not if I have to rough up women, I won't."

"No of course not." But he needed to work, she said. Acting energized him—it was more than just a job, it was life, it gave him purpose. "Negotiate, Jim. Think about it."

He sure did miss it, but not on their terms; he was tired of playing lost-world losers and gangsters.

As Jim lamented his lack of artistic freedom, a second story emerged, courtesy of Moishe: two or three months ago he slept with Melissa. Don't ask why, it just happened. "Maybe out of pity, you know? Who knows why we do half the shit we do. Anyway, it didn't mean anything to me." Well, wouldn't you know it, Melissa gave Moishe the clap and he got treated with the new wonder drug penicillin G and he told her to do the same and then decided she needed something else in life: guidance, leadership, love outside of fucking, and took her in. He felt so guilty about her predicament and fucking her—he just had to make amends, you know? So she stays with him and lives under a regimen of discipline, eating the right foods, exercising, and educating herself. You know everyone in the old neighborhood had their way with her. I'm just giving her a safe house, he said. "Hell, she's reading the Bill of Rights right now. I'm telling you that girl is going to be an informed citizen."

Jim rubbed at the corners of his mouth. "I thought you ran off with her, quit your job, and were hiding out somewhere."

"Here I am. Do I look like I'm hiding? You know her old man makes her do all the dishes? And beat the rugs and scrub the floors—and change the ice in the icebox. I mean, really."

"Yeah. What should I bring tonight?"

"Drinks."

"I don't drink."

"Soft drinks. Missy loves Coke with a little grenadine. She's also crazy about Crayola crayons. The sixteen pack. If you want to get her some of those she'll be happy all night."

Moses handed Jim his card with the home address on it. He told him to bring his wife and maybe they'd play charades with the great Hollywood actor. Jim wasn't sure if Moishe was being ironic. With Moishe you never could tell.

Jim was devoted to the traditions of the theatre and literary arts. He was a serious man, read the work of Nobel Prize–winners such as Romain Rolland who wrote the *Jean Christophe* epic, and the actor believed that Hollywood films, especially in such dark times, ought to do more than offer up hokum and cotton-candy twaddle. Films had a responsibility to reflect back the harsh reality that many working people were dealing with. Instead of the high-minded, Jim's work at Warners was bottom-feeder quality. Most of his films were shot in less than three weeks and featured sensational stories ripped from the headlines. It was depressingly routine. He wanted to play complex people and be in a film with higher production values and something of a "theme." But alas it was just factory art, storylines cut by the yard.

As Billie talked to Moishe and Melissa about life in Hollywood—you can pick oranges right off the tree!—Jim found himself wandering far away, thinking about how to change his persona and expand his repertoire. He had tried to stay engaged in the conversation about F. Scott Fitzgerald, but the game of charades hadn't gone well. Melissa struggled to bring concepts, phrases, famous novels, to life. Her mind just didn't think within certain contours, and Moishe, who insisted on being her partner, kept needling her, asking her off-putting things, like what's the difference between a Pope and a cardinal (the man and the bird), things that didn't really matter, but she couldn't explain.

The sad thing was how close she sat to Moishe, her left arm hooked into his right, her eyes targeted on him. They were moist with love. "I don't understand the book," she said about *The Great Gatsby*, "but I liked it." Her voice was full of canaries, singing in cages.

"Yeah?" Moishe said. "So what's the story about?"

"I don't know. A guy who dies in a pool. But I liked it. It had emotion."

"What kind of emotion?"

"It made me feel sad."

"Sad? Did Nick Carraway make you sad—?"

"Who?"

"The guy telling the story."

"I thought it was Gatsby."

"You don't even understand Fitzgerald's narrative point of view—" He slapped the table with his hand. "Carraway tells the goddamn story."

"Maybe I don't understand everything but the book was great—"

"*Great*? You don't get a thing about it," Moishe said.

"Hey, leave her alone," Jim said.

"Jesus. I thought she was smarter than *that*."

Melissa covered her face and ran into the back bedroom. Earlier in the evening, Moishe yelled at Melissa for dirtying the hand towel in the kitchen and leaving dirt on the bar of soap in the bathroom. "You can't even wash your hands right," he had mumbled. Perhaps Moishe was tiring of Melissa, but all night he attempted to mask his ennui with a perpetual smile at Jim and Billie and a relaxed, lounging posture. Everything Moishe did was lazy and loose—he flopped into chairs, spilled out over the table and other bits of furniture. There was no control to his movements. It was like a Moishe curve ball: sometimes it hit Jim's mitt but far too often it didn't break and plunked left-handed hitters. Whatever the intentions of the dinner party, this wasn't the happy story Moishe promised, that's for sure.

"She gets a kick out of the book, what more do you need? Don't squawk at her." Jim looked over at Billie and then walked into the apartment's lone bedroom. There was but one bed in it.

Melissa was sitting on the edge of the bed, staring at the far wall and a picture of a hand-drawn horse. The horse looked more like a moose and its heavy mane resembled the zigzag line of a set of stairs. "You do that?"

She nodded and refused to look up at him. Her hair was in a tight bun, and her eyes looked like shallow puddles. Her pale green dress had a couple of soup stains from dinner around the frill collar.

"Don't be mad at me," she said.

"I'm not mad at you. The horse is good." He would never have the heart to shoot a horse that was that wonderfully goofy looking.

"I don't want to go back to my dad, Jim." Melissa's breasts were imperceptible in the loose fitting dress she wore. On a walnut dresser to the left of the bed were some crayons worn down like stubby cigars. A rubber ball and seven or eight jacks circled around the feet of a wind-up tin clown seemingly holding a mouse aloft in the air. The mouse was having fun.

"I'm not going to force you." He asked if he could sit next to her.

"When Moishe yells at me, he doesn't mean anything, you know? He just wishes I could hold my own with him. And then maybe we could be a real couple." She grabbed one of the pillows on the bed and showed it to Jim. "We got that in Niagara Falls." Embroidered over an image of Horseshoe Falls in Niagara was some kind of paean to mother and dad and a "token of their love."

"Uh-huh." Jim looked into the bright blinding chrome of the dresser. Cigarettes, hotel matches, and several loose sheets of paper formed a little teepee against the mirror.

"Things pretty tough back home?" Jim picked up the loose leaves and read them. One of them had a score on it in stern ink: 12/20.

She nodded.

"Want to tell me about it?"

"Not really?"

"Come on." He patted her left wrist, propping the sheets of paper back against the mirror's glass. "I'm a good listener." He was. As an actor he prided himself in having control over his body and listening on stage as if it were the first time he had ever heard the words.

A third story: Melissa's dad wasn't a mean man, but he took her for granted, making her do all the cleaning and cooking and never letting her feel special. It was as if she had nothing to offer the world. With Moishe she was learning to draw, to paint, to read, to appreciate the arts. "I know the horse ain't any great shakes, but I—I—"

"It doesn't matter what it is—it makes you feel—well, a sense of accomplishment."

She agreed, worrying her upper lip.

"How'd you like to live with me and Billie in California?"

"You're going back?"

"Probably." It was the first time he admitted it to himself.

"I love New York and I love Moishe."

"Yeah."

She nodded. Her upturned nose had a shiny spot on it. "I don't think you should have pushed that grapefruit in that woman's face."

Jim laughed. "My wife doesn't think so either."

"Grapefruits are medicinal—"

"Yeah, I guess they are—"

"Moishe says I should eat grapefruit 'cause they're medicinal and help control my weight—"

"Your weight? You're at least five pounds under what you should be—"

"Grapefruits are full of vitamins, and now people won't think they're so good for you."

He held up her chin. "If anything, Melissa, the 'grapefruit massage' in *Public Enemy* has got folks eating more grapefruits than ever before."

"Do you like grapefruits?"

"Yes."

"I like them. A lot." She turned away and said she felt like that mouse in the hands of that tin clown, only her father couldn't hold on, he dropped her.

"What?" She was talking metaphors and Jim pushed her to explain.

Many times, more than she could count, her father, to help pay the bills and offset his poker-game debts, had loaned Missy out to some of the boys, including delivery drivers who brought coal and ice. "Don't be mad at me."

The phrase was so child-like. *Don't be mad at me.* Jim squeezed her hand and pinched his teeth against his lower lip. "Your da ain't going to have any say in this or your future—I promise you that." He kissed her forehead. "And I'm not mad at you, Sweetie. You never make me mad."

And then he felt a sharp burn of recognition in his

lower back as he thought about the jacks, the falling mouse, the crayons, and how a couple of summers ago Brother Harry, a doctor, had told Jim about a strange case he'd treated at Bellevue—a woman in her early twenties who looked twelve, forever young, because she had been repeatedly assaulted by her pa since she had turned eight or nine and as a result had never grown up. "Peter Pan limbo," Dr. Harry called it, and now Jim wondered about Melissa. Had her father—? When he'd been drinking?

The burn worked its way behind Jim's eyes and he coughed back tears, and she pointed at his lips, saying don't, and he felt it was all so futile, his career, her life— he had tried to change both and was getting nowhere; sure, he'd return to Hollywood, no better off than when he left, still playing the same characters, but he had been unable to rescue her, and then she touched his lips again, quieting him, and they hugged, and when she started to cry that made Jim loathe his inability to shape and control the world, his, hers, and then, strangely, impulsively, they both laughed, awkwardly child-like, foreheads touching, before one of them suggested that they ought to return to the party. Once they were in the kitchen Jim handed Billie a dollar and asked her to take Melissa out for some ice cream. There was a parlor around the corner, half a block down. "I want to talk to Moishe. Fella-to-fella talk."

"I'm not hungry," Melissa said, looking at Moishe.

"You can go," he nodded. "But just one scoop." He held up a crooked finger.

She nodded back as she and Billie prepared to leave.

It took Melissa five minutes to decide between two pairs of pumps. Once they left, Jim turned to Moishe and rapidly tapped his fingers on the tabletop.

Moishe scheduled Missy's itinerary, day-to-day. When she was showing Jim her pillow from Niagara Falls, he had read a sheet on the bedroom dresser, featuring such things as the time to wake up (7:15 a.m.), what to have for breakfast (two eggs, two pieces of dry toast, half a grapefruit), what to read (*Great Gatsby*, *Young Lonigan*), when to practice musical scales and warm ups (for the blues harp, mid-afternoon), and exercises (isometrics, calisthenics, and small-weight training). It was rigorous. Next to the list Jim also glimpsed a Bill of Rights test Moishe had given her and the low score. "Work harder on comprehension!!" Moishe scrawled across the top of the page in bright, angry ink.

"This isn't going to work," Jim said. "She'll run away from you at some point." He flexed his fingers into another fist.

"My favorite bit in *Public Enemy*? The monstrous keg of beer the size of a V-8 Ford on the dining room table and you guys all sitting around it, straining, trying to see each other. It's surreal—"

"Don't change the subject."

"I give her more than her father. I give her an education. I treat her decently. What more can that girl want?" And if she ran away, so be it, but at least the time spent with him now would give her strength down the road to deal with life.

"You're fucking her."

"I swear—my hand to God—I'm not—"

"There's one bed in the room—"

"We curl up together. She's like a kid, a kid needing attention. I stroke her hair and she curls up like a baby in the womb. My hand to God."

Tomorrow Jim would talk to Johnson Coors and give one of the best performances of his life: smooth, controlled, full of tempered aggression. He wouldn't be Tom Powers. Instead, he would be a shy, retiring fella, persuasively telling the father to leave his daughter alone. She was on her own now and if you want the authorities to hear about you prostituting her, well, they will. No more contact, savvy?

"You're a benign dictator, Moishe. She even had to ask for permission to leave the apartment. And one scoop of ice cream? For chrissakes."

"Oh, come on. I'm making her life meaningful."

"By demeaning her for not understanding a novel?"

"You know you should read *Young Lonigan*—it would be a great part for you."

"I've read it." Studs Lonigan *would* be a good part. Jim rubbed at his upper lip. "You gave her the clap, didn't you?"

"What?"

"That's why you're doing all this."

"I don't have sex with her, and I've sworn off the boys." It was as if he too sought an existence in a pure childlike state and perhaps Melissa was helping him. Moishe had always felt guilty and dirty over being a "fairy" and now, maybe, it was a non-issue. He no longer disliked himself, he said. "We do wonders for each other."

"Yeah, I can see that. Wonders, uh-huh. Took her

five minutes to figure out what shoes to wear."

He exhaled sharply off his cigarette. "But she got it right, didn't she? The green ones. They match her dress and accessories—handbag, compact." You don't understand, he said, it was true, he had given her the clap, but he was doing penance now and felt good about helping her. He wished the poor girl wouldn't love him so much, but he was improving her quality of life. He had genuine affection for her, but that's all he could have. "We made love just that one time." Ashes dripped from his cigarette. "She keeps hoping for more, but that's not what this is about." It was like a Chekhov story, he said, where someone does something bad, immoral, and then tries to rectify the situation, amend his mistakes by doing the right thing, making a difference.

"Which Chekhov story is that?" Jim asked. He liked Chekhov—admired the even-handed tone to his work, the lack of judgment to his voice and his sensitivity for the human condition. Warners would never make a film based off a Chekhov story. And if they opted on *Young Lonigan* there would surely be several indiscriminate rounds of fire from chattering Tommy guns. "Come on, name one. Name a Chekhov story."

"I don't know. It just sounded good." Moishe paused and took a slow drag. "Shit. I guess I should've said Tolstoy. But I never did like Tolstoy. How about you?"

"There's a lot of things I don't like," said Jim.

Written on the Sky

HE SKY IN TORONTO IS A KIND OF BLUE THAT'S so different from anywhere else I've been, especially the Midwest—Kansas, Illinois, and now Iowa—where I teach playwriting and script analysis. I don't know if it's all the farms and humidity that make the blue of Iowa not quite as bright, but in Toronto it's almost an opaque powdery blue, the calm comfort of faded jeans.

I'm sure I didn't really think that way about it when I was a kid, but the backyard sky was something that protected me, an umbrella that hid me from the nuclear ash of my parents' bitter arguments. They fought all the time and often Dad—perpetually angry with my mother—deflected his dinner table rage on me, calling me Hoover, the big galoot who sucked up food like a human vacuum cleaner. When not wincing me with words, he'd whack my face for being lippy. But in the recesses of our backyard, I invented scenes of escape, comical set pieces: the Lone Ranger on the take; John Wayne trying to sing "Bang a Gong"; and my Macedonian grandpa, in his thick European accent, struggling to explain the nuances of offsides in hockey to a grandson. I guess I never did have many friends, outside of those I scripted.

Anyway, by backyard hedges I dreamed of disappearing into sky, writing something as great as *The Honeymooners*—I mean like really writing on the sky: my words chiseled marks, like a Mark VII logo hammered onto the closing credits of *Dragnet*. Hell, in our family we never watched Masterpiece Theatre or anything on PBS. *Get Smart, All in the Family,* and all shows produced by Jack Webb were what were on in our home.

Mrs. Casson, our neighbor, often heard me doing some bit like the time I was Superman getting his secret powers from matzo crackers and gefilte fish, and then she'd laugh and offer me a Coke (never from a can, always a glass bottle), or a triangle of French cheese, or rye bread slashed with pâté. She loved international foods. "A woman's got to dream of getting away, doesn't she?" she once said, by way of explanation. She smelled of Coppertone and vanilla and I never saw her husband. He was a disc jockey on easy listening CFRB, but like I said, I never saw him.

Many an afternoon she suntanned on a lawn recliner and asked me real questions—not what I wanted to be when I grow up or how much do I weigh or what grade am I going into—but explorations of meaning that my father never invested in: Is there something beyond that vast blue—alien civilizations? Multiple gods? What would it be like to write on the sky and use the clouds as erasers?

It felt good to be around her. I was only thirteen the summer that Jack Tremblay moved in with us, but I sure felt something in Mrs. Casson's presence. It was a want that traveled like prickly cattails through my heart and fingers.

Mrs. Casson smiled, and then laid on her chest, against the green recliner, her bikini top unstrapped.

I thought Mrs. Casson was pretty and even went so far as to tell my mom that our neighbor had a nice figure. "Oh, really? Mrs. Casson? Why, she's all shoulders and her ass is too big. Her proportions are all wrong." And then she said the ultimate insult for a 1950s woman (although this was 1974, my mom came of age in an era of curves and rockabilly): "She looks mannish." Damn, my mother loved commenting on other people's looks, especially actors in old movies. She noticed which ones had puffy eyes from too much drinking and who wore a rug, pointing out where the real and synthetic weaves broke in different directions. Ray Milland was a favorite object of ridicule. "Cary Grant–lite" she called him. I never could see what she was talking about.

Outside of critiquing people's looks, Mom was pretty generous. She always gave me a leftover dollar to buy hockey cards, *Mad* magazine, or candy bars. And every Halloween she traveled door-to-door with two orange and black boxes collecting for UNICEF. She even made all the costumes for our fourth-grade play, a jazz variant on *Snow White*. I played a dwarf.

Throughout seventh grade (the last school year before Mrs. Casson moved away), Mom often signed me out early from Woodbine Junior High under the pretense of a doctor or dentist's appointment. She knew I was struggling—not with school; I was an "A" student, but the social stuff. I was sad after Nancy—our Snow White in the jazz musical—moved to, of all places,

Montreal. I had a crush on her since way back in second grade. She was one of those girls who hit a softball farther than you and you didn't hate her for it because she was girly in other ways: wearing blue dresses and laughing at your jokes. In fifth grade, she loved how I said "faucet" with a hard "k" for the "c."

Anyway, Jack Tremblay, who was staying with us that final summer with Mrs. Casson next door, often had a beer in his hand and smoked in the backyard so that he could talk to our neighbor before the red sky darkened. "Why don't you play 500?" he'd say to me. "Looks like Mo Frazier could use someone to shag flies." An open lake of green spread between our townhouse and the public school, and there was Mo (Maurice to his mother), a doctor's kid with a bat resting against his left shoulder. Reluctantly I hustled after each fly ball, this one hitting me in the shoulder, that one on my hip, another against my knees. Through the scratches of sky—dandelion puffs and bits of dust kicked up most nights—Jack leaned on hedges, a hand at the side of his chin, his head bent in a tableau of listening. Mrs. Casson, knees together, nodded, following the thread of his words, but her shoulders were square, pulling her back. I couldn't help but notice how when Jack was around her, the bikini top was never unclasped.

"Hey, dumbass, that's the fifth fly you've muffed," Mo said, his spiky hair looking like a surrealist landscape. I chucked that ball at his head, but it arced awkwardly, twisting twenty feet to his left.

Maurice cursed me. He was always Jesus Christing something. His father, like mine, was rarely home. His mom, Doris, I learned years later, was a closet alcoholic. She was my mom's best friend and they often shared coffee and personal stories. Anyway, everyone in the neighborhood knew about her drinking, I guess, but no one could do anything to help her. She directed our jazz musical and told us to watch Carol Burnett. "She never breaks. This play is funny, but if you laugh you ruin the fun for the audience. You want to laugh, buy a ticket and watch it from the front row." She also promoted the virtues of margarine over butter, whole-wheat noodles over white, and water over Kool-Aid. She wasn't a lot of fun, but she was healthy—except for the drinking part. That must have been her Carol Burnett moment; the control she had to present around us, all the time.

"Mo, don't curse so much. The wind caught Graham's throw," Mrs. Casson said, giving me a big thumbs-up. Through the gauzy scratches of twilight, I waved back and promised myself to do better.

"Doesn't he look like Johnny Cash," she asked Jack.

"Yeah. I guess I can see it a little."

"A little? Look at the eyes—"

The next fly ball somehow caught the center webbing of my glove.

ONE HOT SUMMER AFTERNOON WHEN I WAS TWELVE— the kind of afternoon that burns the edges of your shoulders and gives the space between grass and sky a crinkly weave—Jack and my father took me to the bachelors' pad. They were three guys who shared a townhouse and enjoyed lounging at the compound's pool, drinking dark beers in plastic cups, and checking out the girls and flirting with other men's wives. All three were in their mid-twenties and sold cars. My dad thought they were "pretty cool dudes."

Anyway, the year before when Dad was unemployed he had gotten to know Mark Holmes, the leader of the posse. They had planned for months to go into a pool cleaning business, but Mark, according to Mom, "got cold feet. He's just a kid."

This particular afternoon when I was twelve, Mark couldn't believe it when one of the other bachelors announced that he had slept with Lynn (that's Mrs. Casson. Although she gave me permission to call her by her first name I never called her Lynn. I don't know why. It just didn't feel right). *Slept.* I kind of knew what it meant—it was more than just blankets and bodies intertwined and when Jack pumped his fist twice and said, "Solid, Jackson," I knew it was serious stuff. Hell, maybe I *did* know what Bachelor Number Two meant, but I didn't want to believe it. "Right there in the kitchen, huh?" Jack asked.

My father's laughter was a coughing cacophony. It rumbled deep in his stomach and barreled through his chest, making his face and shoulders shake. When something really cracked him up, he raised a hand as if asking an umpire for time out. His hand was again up, doing the asking. "I'm not touching any of the leftovers." He pointed at the refrigerator door. "Let me tell you that much."

Sure, Dad could be rough with me, but when laughing, dark crescent moons for eyes, he was fun to be around. When I was five, Dad told me that he and Jack were WWII heroes, a submarine commander and his

Chief Petty Officer (I never knew what that meant but it had to be important). Well, some Nazi schweinhund blew up their sub and Jack and Dad seized hold of fuselage remnants and floated twenty miles of ocean to an island of coconuts. "See, see, kid? My right arm, to this day, is longer than my left. That's 'cause I was swimming with this here arm." How was I to know that from 1939-45 my father was between the ages of two and eight?

Jack, even that summer when I was thirteen, enjoyed laughing alongside Pop, embellishing their stories about work (fellow milkmen stealing from the company), transvestites at the bar (dancing with unsuspecting college kids), or forlorn women at the track (looking to be "rescued"). "I don't have a drinking problem," Jack periodically repeated that summer. "I have a problem staying sober." That seemed to be the funniest line ever. Apparently Tillie, Jack's wife, didn't find it so funny, asking him to quit drinking or to quit her. Like I said, I don't think I ever saw him without a beer, especially during Saturdays' Hockey Night in Canada broadcasts.

But I liked Jack. He let me have the first sips off of freshly opened bottles and he made the coolest paper airplanes. I don't know how he did it. His didn't look like mine, flying evergreens, all razor-sharp and pointed. Instead, he folded the paper in such a way as to create replicas of bush pilot planes flown by WWI aviators. And they dipped and skipped like flat stones through air.

The sky, the afternoon we visited the bachelors, was excruciatingly bright and hurt my eyes, but the lights inside were dim. Extra beers, the ones they couldn't fit in their refrigerator, were parked along a kitchen counter.

The soldiers had different labels and were probably imported. There were also two floor lamps in the room, a couple of low slung couches covered in crocheted throws, and a solid-state television topped with ashtrays full of crumpled cigarettes.

But I wasn't really looking at all that. On the walls were photographs of naked women. I couldn't really tell you the color of the walls, because of all the centerfolds upon centerfolds. I knew about *Playboy*. Mo and I had snuck glances at the magazine resting high on the rack—by the bread and deli aisle—of our local IGA. In the store, our gazes were quick, looking for the floor manager while still looking at the girls, but now, I couldn't believe I was allowed to stare at all that beauty. I felt for sure someone was going to scold or hit me.

"What do you think, huh?" My father nudged Mark as if to say, check out the kid. Mark smiled, his bleached hair matching the color of his skin. A giant peace chain dipped around his neck like a gold anchor. "Pretty cool dudes, huh?" Dad elbowed me gently.

"Pretty cool," I think I echoed. What struck me were the highly noticeable tan lines. There was something about those borders, faded lines against darker accents on white bodies that suggested a peering into the forbidden. The lighter swatches teased you with the promise of more to see: a mystery revealed while still remaining veiled. I felt a yearning I never knew before. "What's her name?"

A model relaxed by a pool. A soft drink was in some kind of Styrofoam holder and her legs were crossed, backside exposed, and chin cupped in her hands as she looked at me. Her un-tanned butt was bright. I pointed her out from the ten or so models close by.

Mark laughed. "What, you want her phone number, killer?"

My stomach was full of rocks.

My father examined the photograph on the wall. "That's Sharon Clark."

"Nice ass," Jack said.

"Not as good as the ass I got last night," Bachelor Number Two said.

"So I hear." Jack smiled back. "She's not a ball-breaker is she? After my wife, I don't want no more ball-breakers."

"No. Very smooth. Like a glass of Crown Royal."

The rocks suddenly dissolved into pebbly shards, fluttering about in my stomach, as I feared not my Mom catching me looking but Mrs. Casson finding out. I didn't want her to know that I was looking at these girls and hearing these words, because I knew she held me in such high regard. Several months before, while sharing some cannoli she had ordered from the French Quarter in New Orleans, she said I wasn't like most twelve year olds. "You're what we called in my day eccentric. But I now call interesting." I was arty, into the deeper meanings of things. "Some people learn that blue is a relaxing color, but you, Graham, you want to know why blue and not red or turquoise." I smiled, and she fell back in the lawn recliner, her arms triangles above her head. And that's when I told her I wanted to be a writer for a show like *The Honeymooners*. You notice how Alice never attacks Ralph? She only responds to his attacks. She never attacks first.

"Maybe she should," Mrs. Casson said. "Maybe she ought not be that nice. I'm not nice."

I wanted to tell her that she was, but instead babbled something about the candy dish on the show, the one lonely sign of a woman's life in their apartment, and how it must have been something Alice placed there to brighten up the place, and her life.

But on that particular day with the bachelors, my father, and Jack, I wasn't thinking about candy dishes. Instead, I felt shame and guilt for thinking about women in ways I had vaguely approached.

"Crown Royal? Guys c'mon, huh? Keep it above board. The kid?" Dad touched my shoulders.

"Sharon Clark," I repeated to alleviate the tension. I often did that. I appeared clumsy to many. Hell, alongside "Hoover," Dad's favorite nickname for me was Max, as in Maxwell Smart, Secret Agent 86, because I was always stumbling about. I'd come in from playing ball hockey or baseball outside and trip in the door's entryway. And at the kitchen table, I can't tell you how many times I knocked over a glass of juice. But in social situations I had some grace. I read people well—moods, disappointments, recriminations. I know when to be funny, when to deflect a situation. So I returned to the poolside Ms. Clark. "I tell you what. Wow. With a glow-in-the-dark butt like that who needs a night light, huh?"

At the time, I was still using one.

"Good one, kid. Good one." And the men all laughed.

WHEN I WAS SIX, I SAW A LIVE CHILDREN'S SHOW WITH

Mom at the O'Keefe Centre and all the way home was sulking in the car. "What, you didn't like it?" she asked. "No, no." I couldn't quite articulate it, but I didn't like sitting. I wanted to be up on stage with the other performers. I wanted to be in the show. Not a spectator. I think Mrs. Casson knew that about me and sometime after our conversation about Audrey Meadows, she invited me into her home. It smelled of flowers and fresh bread and the colors were all bright yellows and pastel pinks. In her basement was a huge chest that I expected to overflow with doubloons and pieces of eight. But it was crammed with costumes, wigs, hair extensions, and theatrical props like fans, parasols, and pistols.

Mrs. Casson wanted to be an actress. Well, as a matter of fact she was an actress and had done some indie shows in downtown Toronto, but her husband didn't like other men looking at her and asked her to retire. So she did. "I don't know why I listened to him." She placed a hand on the side of her face and looked out into the backyard. "I guess I was in love." She laughed and placed a scepter in her right hand. "Oh, well, too late for a comeback."

That first afternoon we relived a scene from *Henry IV, Part 1*. She was Hal, me Falstaff. I don't remember the particulars, but it had something to do with the players playacting conversations in a mood of comic relief that would later be played out for real. I felt immortal, no longer afraid of messing up, of flubbing a ground ball or hitting myself in the forehead while dribbling a basketball. With Mrs. Casson there was no self-consciousness. On subsequent summer afternoons, I was Mitch to her Blanche Dubois or we set aside the classics, often writing or improvising our own scripts. She made pirate hats out of paper—well, they actually looked more like something Robin Hood would sport, but I didn't say anything about that—and we'd imagine ourselves on the Seven Seas, but instead of carousing and robbing other ships, we offered to make fellow seafarers laugh by putting on a show. She'd slide into a pair of tap shoes and then hit the floor with repeated gun bursts. "A tap dancer is but a frustrated drummer," she once said in a middle of a rousing rat-a-tat-tat. And I'd sing some kind of self-penned rock 'n' roll song. One was called "Watergate" and featured such pithy lyrics as: "It started with a Washington cocktail / and then it got carried away / until it went to the president / of the USA / Watergate, Watergate."

Afternoon flowed into afternoon and we traveled beyond sky to worlds where aliens ate cheese and drew animals that resembled horses in the margins of their weekly stock reports. It was fun and there were no rules. She even kissed me on the cheek once, because her character had been in an asylum for two years and was finally set free. I was her younger brother and on the way home stopped off at a Dairy Queen because she was unable to get any of that in the asylum. At the time, I didn't think about subtexts. Did Mrs. Casson feel trapped in an asylum in real life? Now, I wonder. Anyway, back then we were outside of judgment, just following each other's impulses, living, being.

FROM WHAT I SAW, JACK WAS GENTLE AROUND MY MOM.

About Mrs. Casson he'd blurt about blunt things, like he wished he were a truck driver and how he'd ball her jack. But I never heard an unkind word about my mother. Every night, after dinner, he helped wash and dry the dishes. "Hell, a woman's work may never be done, but us men folk can sure give a hand." It was so cornball but damn sincere.

So imagine my surprise when I came home from a long bike ride into the bright suburbs (I often did that—writing stories while riding) to discover Jack and his two suitcases and paper airplanes were gone. He was no longer living on the cot in the basement. Had he worked things out with Tillie?

"What do you know about Tillie?" Mom shook her head and said I ought to mind my own beeswax.

So, I went and asked my father, who was spread across the couch watching another Audie Murphy Western.

"I left his bags on the front stoop for him to take," Dad said, his left hand shielding his eyes from the television's brightness. "And he took them."

OVER THE YEARS, I OFTEN WONDERED WHY IT WAS that Jack left so unceremoniously and it wasn't until my early forties, and following my parents' divorce, that my mother told me that Jack had made a pass at her. She didn't reveal all the details, but here's what I was able to puzzle out:

Jack, tired from just having talked with Tillie over the phone, slunk into a chair by the kitchen table. His wife blamed Tommy (my dad) for Jack's excessive drinking and staying out all hours. She even insisted on Jack passing the phone to Frances (my mom) so Tillie could cast aspersions on Mom's inability to control Tommy. Jack wouldn't let her. "Tom's not to blame. I make my choices." "Tommy is to blame. And Frances." "No, you are. You don't even want to make love." "I don't want to make love to a man who smells like a distillery." "Bullshit." "Well, bullshit right back at you." Jack laughed at that last comment and Tillie hung up. "Tillie sends her regards."

"She blames Tom for your drinking—"

"Pay no attention." He held up a hand. "She's upset. She'll say anything. It's everyone else's fault but hers." He looked at his fingers. "I drink because I want to. I choose to."

"Maybe you shouldn't drink so much."

"Maybe I shouldn't do a lot of things."

"What does that mean?"

"Nothing."

Then I imagine my mother looked away, ladling broth over her roast. With a roast she often mixed up a side dish of cucumbers, cumin, and sour cream, and she probably prepared that right then to distract herself. "She ought not to call here. If she expects to talk to me—" The tops of her arms were shaking.

"You're right. She shouldn't harass you." He leaned back and wondered when Tommy would return from Vic Tanney's, a local gym.

"Why didn't you join him?"

He arched his back, sticking out his beer gut, hitting it with his fists as if it were a giant floor tom. "I like the way I look." He laughed. "She thought we were—?" He looked up at her and then back into his cup of coffee. "Coffee's the perfect drink, you know? It's food in a cup."

"You want me to freshen up your cup?"

"No."

"You mean, because Tom's not here, Tillie thought—?"

"Yes." He sipped at his coffee. "I mean, I wouldn't even think of it unless—"

"No."

"Right."

Anyway, that was it. That one overture, and the next afternoon Jack's two bags were sitting on the front stoop, waiting for him.

I imagine Dad was not only furious but didn't want to hear from Mom how the pass was but a vague drive-by quip. Dad didn't see moral issues in shades of gray. It was all cut and dried. A man makes a pass at your wife: he's no longer a friend. Maybe Mom, in defending Jack, mentioned how every morning construction workers whistled at her from the bus stop to her place of work or how dark-complected men with darker hair shouted their affections through open streetcar windows. Men are always on the make. "I should know."

"Know what?"

"I see how you look at Lynn."

"Lynn? Are you nuts? That girl suntans way too much. Her skin's darker than an unpeeled potato."

Mom and Dad argued even more after Jack was gone. The phony truce between them was broken. They no longer minded their manners and if I spilled juice at the table I got smacked pretty good.

Mom knew I needed to escape all that, so she often drove me away from the school to the early autumn of downtown Toronto where we caught a matinee. I loved old films, the ones CBC would show on Fridays starring Bogart or Cagney, and I liked Woody Allen because he liked Bogart and his films were funny. So we walked among the crisp gold and red leaves and later saw movies like *Play it Again, Sam*; *Bananas*; and *Sleeper*.

But on this particular day, two weeks after Jack left, Mom's mood was off. She was eating a giant-sized hamburger from McDonald's and slurping back a soft drink that looked like a can of oil. Mom hated junk food. She offered me a fry and then the remains of her hamburger. "You want a bite?"

"No thanks."

She worried her right hand along the top of the steering wheel while speeding south on the Don Valley, grits of food sputtering from her lips. "Lynn's a bitch. A real bitch."

Mom never used that word. I stared out the passenger window, watching the guardrail posts zip by like plastic pegs on a Lite-Brite board.

Just the previous weekend, I had returned from a soccer game to find Mrs. Casson catching one of her last tans of the season. It was getting too cool to keep it up much longer. Anyway, she asked me to rub suntan lotion on her lower back, reaching places she couldn't. I lowered and rubbed between shoulder blades, down to her bra strap. Her shoulders weren't tense at all. I had figured since she too was in a bad marriage her back would feel all knotted up but it was smooth.

165

"You don't like school, huh?" The stiff fabric of the chaise muffled her voice.

"I do all right."

"Stay with school." I was too sensitive, too smart, to not become a college professor or something. Mrs. Casson also told me that she dropped out after tenth grade. She was chronically shy and would get "nervous bumps" in her stomach or at least that's how it felt.

"You were shy?"

"Surprised?"

"Yes."

"Today I was looking into the sky and imagined myself dissolving into all that blue. Like an Alka-Seltzer tablet in a glass, you know? I know that image isn't the prettiest, but that's how I felt. Bubbles popping, hissing, and then no more."

I quit kneading the lotion and sat closer to her, wanting to reassure her that the world would not be a better place without her, but I didn't have the words and mumbled something about how there had to be something beyond darkness. Mrs. Casson didn't think we ever died. From energy we came and to energy we become. In the end, we enter the cosmos as a pulsing force, providing the light of wisdom for others. "This I truly believe," she said, and then she pictured a distant future, the two of us writing across a bone dry sky, sparking bubbles of hope for others.

And then she said, "I'm sorry, I talk too much," and her eyes were wet.

"Breaking up homes." Mom now stopped across from the theatre and yanked on the parking brake.

Breaking up homes. I knew what that meant. My Mom and I had watched a lot of Barbara Stanwyck and Bette Davis movies. "Mrs. Casson and Jack?"

"No, not Mrs. Casson and Jack. No!" She slapped the top of the steering wheel with the undersides of her hands.

The rest of the afternoon was surreal. "Let's see some arty shit," Mom announced. This was a woman who loved Ingmar Bergman and now she was calling art cinema shit and eating hamburgers. Anyway, we watched *A Woman Under the Influence* directed by John Cassavetes, and it was bizarre for a thirteen-year-old to behold. It was nothing like the sitcoms or cop shows on mainstream TV. The protagonist, a lady who was a bit of a kookaboo (mentally unstable I would now call her), had all these shifts in moods and let the kids in her care run free and naked about her house. Her husband slapped her around and *she* gets institutionalized for a time. Before they take her away she sings to her husband—the Columbo guy—and his friends and it's real awkward and hard-bitten and strange as boundaries of the proper and improper break down. It was the most real experience I ever felt in a theatre for I was watching my own family's histrionics (neuroses, I'd now call it) dancing across a sky of white.

You'd think after what I knew about Mrs. Casson and my father I would never see her again, but life doesn't always play to expectations. With autumn we no longer had weekday afternoons, but I found time on weekends to visit. Maybe I wanted answers, a direct apology, but I never asked her about the affair.

I never asked my father either.

To tell you the truth, I was a little jealous about what happened between Mrs. Casson and my father. I know, it sounds like some goddamn Oedipal drama, but that wasn't the issue. I didn't want to sleep with Mrs. Casson, but our relationship was more than just a childhood crush or infatuation. Around her I was more myself than I was in the presence of my father (and my mother). With Mrs. Casson I felt an overwhelming sadness that I wanted to extinguish from both of us.

Mom worried about me spending time at Mrs. Casson's. She never said anything directly; it was all subtext: a downward look, a distracted shrug, a quick gasp of air. "Always about her looks with the damn suntanning. Doesn't she ever work?" Sometimes, I wondered if Dad had told Mom all about taking me to see the Playmates on the bachelor walls because Mom often placed Lynn within that landscape.

Anyway, my games with Mrs. Casson weren't as spirited as they were before the affair and often took a downbeat turn. Our narratives were now about alienation, loneliness, and sadness. Our heroes lacked direction, shifting through settings. With no clear goals we drifted from one situation to another. On one afternoon we traveled to another planet and forgot all about returning to Earth. It just didn't matter anymore. And she never did tap dance again.

To counter her blue moods, I often suggested we do something funny so we dusted off Neil Simon's *The Odd Couple* and she was a very fastidious Felix, ad-libbing lines, complaining about the smell of burned leaves in my hair or how the tag to my Lees was sticking out above the denim. I liked playing Oscar.

"Don't say the lines the way they're written. Say them how you feel." She shrugged her shoulders. "Words—they're just suggestions." She lit a cigarette. "How do you intersect with this character?"

I don't know. I'm messy I guess. Disorganized. I wanted to tell her that my writing was changing. What I scrawled on yellow legal pads were no longer parodies of Superman and the Lone Ranger. Instead, a sexual subtext was filling in at the edges of my sitcoms, including one about a liberal, single mother, a high school drama teacher, and her son, an NDP voter, sexually conservative, and recent graduate from the University of Toronto, who is struggling to find full-time employment and thus returns "home" to live with her. They fight about everything, especially her romances with younger men. The opening scene to the pilot begins with his unexpected arrival. Mom opens the door to find her son standing there, men's briefs (not his own) dangling from his hand. "I guess some things never change," he says. Years later, that opening scene evolved into my first produced play, *Honest Goodbye.*

So, unable to express what I wanted to tell her, I changed the subject. "How about you? How do you intersect with your character?"

She hesitated, playing with the delicate buttons on her blouse. "I don't. I'm channeling Tony." That was her husband.

I wanted to ask why he was never around but kids

don't always feel like they have the right to ask such questions. So I just nodded my head like I understood, feeling the gap between me and adulthood was years away from closing.

THE FOLLOWING SPRING, AFTER THE HOLIDAYS, MRS. Casson had moved to Burlington. Years later, I was working on a play, my fifth, set in 1964 about a World War II vet and drifter who works at the foundry and falls for a woman dying of Parkinson's, when I heard that Lynn Casson had died from skin cancer. At her funeral were twenty or so people, including myself and Doris Frazier and her young son from a second marriage. The eulogy failed to bring alive any of Lynn's complexities, her desperate need to be loved, to be understood. Afterward, I joined Doris for coffee and we rekindled Lynn stories and how one New Year's Eve, dressed in a parka imported from Russia, Lynn danced in her backyard to Beatles tunes.

My father died of brain cancer last April.

I know nothing of Jack Tremblay's life or whereabouts.

My mother experienced a stroke, two years ago Labor Day. Afterward she began reinventing her life, conjuring up new stories that didn't jibe with the past. For example, she'd brag to my wife how I was brought up in a "cultured" household, listening to the "classics": Billie Holiday and John Coltrane. Really? The beat of my childhood can be traced to the soundtrack of *Easy Rider*, the choogle of Creedence Clearwater Revival, and the anxiety-laden depression of the Moody Blues's *Days of*

Future Past.

Just the other day, Mom told my oldest girl Annie that the large stuffed tiger sitting on top of Grandma's dresser had been something she saved her allowance money up for a whole year and bought for $125 when she was fourteen. Again, really? Since I was eight, Mom told me Dad bought her that tiger during their honeymoon, New York City 1956. Mom's nickname for Dad was "Tiger." I guess the past gift must've felt like some residual hold over her that she wanted to be free of, so she revised history for a new narrative about frugality and patience.

These latter day revisions got me to thinking: What if my mother has always been revising stories? What if instead of just the imaginative wanderings of Lynn and me and the games we played on hot afternoons, Mom too was a fanciful storyteller?

"You never had much of a childhood, did you?" Doris said that afternoon we went out for coffee. What with all the fighting and tension and marital unhappiness, your mother said it made you retreating, distant from others, guarded. "I don't know, I guess you were just born old, Graham."

"That's from a movie," I said to change the subject, and then Doris told me that her husband had since passed and Maurice was now a corporate lawyer out in Vancouver. Doris also said that she had beaten alcohol and it showed: her face was much brighter, less pulled down with the weight of liquor. Then I told her about Mom's failing health, misaligned stories about the tiger, and Lynn's affair with my father in 1974. Doris nodded and solemnly reached for my hand, reciprocating in the way that one intimacy leads to another, telling me about Frances and Jack. My mother needed gentleness and appreciation and to be loved. Doris's re-telling was vague, full of gaps, but the "day of the pass" went something like this:

"Can you believe that, my wife thought—?" Jack looked down at the scuffed marks on his shoes and shrugged.

"Why not think that?" According to Doris, Frances tossed silverware into the sink and it clattered like a thousand clacking marbles. What do people think of us anyway? My mother wondered. This family? She shook her head. Before Jack came to live with them, Tom often abused Fran and Graham with cruel shouts, upended furniture, and flourishes of anger, broken objects: plates, radios, curtain rods. Where had the tenderness gone?

And poor Graham—the repeated slaps to his face and words hurled upon his psyche had become such a dinnertime occurrence that the boy had started asking if he could eat in the living room, in front of the TV. He said it was to watch reruns of *Run for Your Life* and *Perry Mason*, but Frances knew better. Even at school, Graham was skittish, unconnected to the other kids in his classroom. When he was five, Mrs. Salisbury and Principal Hamilton thought Graham might be mildly retarded so he was sent to a special school for a week. Their findings? He's fine. Get him a dog. A dog? No, he needed a *family*.

Jack touched Frances's shoulders and told her she was a great mom and he'd talk to Tommy and tell him to back off a little and not spend so much money throwing darts in a bar or chasing women at a track. He then grazed the ends of her hair, sweeping some of it off her shoulders, and the sink was no longer crackling with silverware, and Frances wished the sound would return to pause her from kissing Jack.

"I'm a mess," Jack said afterward. "Look at me." He tousled his own hair. "I drink too much." He might stop drinking for a woman like her, but he wouldn't bet on it. He kissed her elbows and the tip of her shoulders and then the bridge of her nose. "I'll talk to Tom."

"Don't bother," she said, the sheet tight under her chin because she was a little embarrassed and shy over what had passed. "He won't change." She offered to make Jack a second cup of coffee.

"Sure," he said.

Perhaps Jack was bitter at my mom's eventual rejection of him and at Tommy for never offering him a chance at clarification. But what was there to clarify really? Perhaps Jack just accepted it all; the same way Lynn accepted her loneliness.

I don't know. It's another story: Doris's words being filtered through me. Is it a truth? Did Mom embellish for Doris or did Mom scale back for me?

Aw, hell. I'm probably just writing against the sky, the way Lynn always wanted me to. Maybe I'll write a play about all this someday and like O'Neill and *Long Day's Journey* have it published three years after I die. I don't know. Perhaps Lynn's with me now as I write these very words, guiding my hand, mourning for us all.

I like to think so anyway.

Still the Bomber

❦

TWO YEARS BEFORE THE COMEBACK, JOHN "THE Bomb" Dreyfuss watched amber light slink away as if a very part of him were disappearing. Daughter Rebekah leaned against the sink, a ginger glass in her left hand, and then dropped the bottle into the basin where it crackled. "I'm tired of this. I'm tired of it." She whipped red hair over a shoulder and shook her head, eyes on the bright laces of her sneakers.

Donna, Dreyfuss's wife, was tired of it all too. From the far end of the Formica table she was lost in inward contemplation. Remnants of a broken radio dotted the floor and spots of plaster dusted the top of a baseboard. Crouched under a retro hi-fi cabinet was Cagney, Dreyfuss's dog, the crook of a paw over his left eye.

Cagney had recently been diagnosed with a partially collapsed trachea—left side—so that whenever he exerted himself he wheezed and folded up with a resigned huff. At twelve he'd lost interest in wobbling up stairs. He was currently not moving.

Two weeks after this incident Donna will have moved out of the house. Three weeks from that date she will have filed for divorce and found a secretarial job with a Santa Cruz construction firm. But during this brief moment, amber drops drained and Dreyfuss felt a wondrous calm as self-definitions disassembled.

"Something needs to change," Donna finally said. "I want you to go to AA. I'm going to set up an intervention."

He laughed. "You don't know the first thing about an intervention. You don't tell the person *about* it before you *do* it." He scoffed, walked to the sink, and touched the broken glass, gently washing fingers to lips.

The room filled with amber diamonds.

His dressing room was the green of heavy molasses. Everything: his desk, the small lights around his makeup mirror, and cards and telegrams of support from fans. Green.

Doctors often ask patients to rank their pain on a scale of one to ten. In the case of Dreyfuss's depression a system of colors applied to his various moods. When he was manic and happy, the world was full of ambers, reds, and whites. When he was down, the world was a spectrum of green, teal, and blue, especially the faded denim of an early morning sky.

It was like this for as long as he could imagine. It was only after he first started drinking as a teenager that the colors for his moods, which were in the beginning merely metaphoric, suddenly became actualized.

Still the Bomber was in its seventh week and there was little improvement in the seriousness of the scripts or upgrade to the stupidity of his character. Producer Michael LeGrand had promised that this would be no mere *Saved by the Bell* moose-ca-ca. In the late 1980s,

Bring on the Bomber was a hip sitcom, retrofitting the original *Leave it to Beaver*. It featured a pubescent kid, Johnny "the Bomb" Lambertino, his older brother Larry (played by Lenny Katz), and their two Moms, Jean and Jane. Each episode was a morality tale as one of Bomber's pals: Frankie "the Christmas Goose" Collins, who ate an apple in every scene, or Chuck Desjardins, a fat kid who often said "That's so stucco" about things he liked, lured the Bomber into a series of wrong choices. Even better yet, he skipped school to rock with the Ramones on MTV Live. In one much ballyhooed episode, Bomber climbed a billboard to see if he could actually sit in the 3-D cup protruding from the sign (the latter was a clear shout out to a classic 1961 *Beaver* adventure, "In the Soup"). Often one of Bomber's moms or his ultra-cool older bro steered the Bomb in the right direction. Each episode ended with a mini-epiphany and the Bomber getting wiser.

Flash-forward thirty years: the Bomb is now forty-two and no wiser than he was at twelve. Filmed before a live studio audience at the Del Mar Theatre in Santa Cruz (a concession LeGrand granted to help keep Dreyfuss out of East LA), this week's episode had Bomber embarrassing his youngest son Lionel when Dad dated the boy's fourth-grade teacher. All the kids ridiculed L-Train, labeling him a teacher's pet. The episode ended with "the Bomb" asking his sixty-four-year-old Mom Jane (Jean had since passed away) for advice.

Lenny poked his head into Dreyfuss's dressing room. "Hey, Amigo, you look a little down. What's up, bro?" He could always read Dreyfuss's moods and the two served

as best man at each other's weddings. Lenny had a narrow face and a receding hairline, featuring what he affectionately labeled in a self-portrait of words as "Larry
Fine with a Jew-fro."

Dreyfuss shrugged and reiterated his frustrations
over the scripts and the development of the show. He
had agreed to return to "quality television," not some
lame-ass sitcom. "I want better stories."

"I dig ya, but we're number seventeen in the ratings,
bubeleh." Besides, the Katz girls (Lenny's wife and two
daughters) loved the show.

"I don't think Rebekah loves it."

"No." Lenny looked away. "No. She calls it 'honky
culture.'"

Why couldn't Rebekah communicate her vitriol with
him instead of Lenny? Ever since her Bat Mitzvah and
Dreyfuss's then escalating booze intake, she had felt
much more comfortable around his best friend. Dreyfuss had never really been there for her or Donna—his
attention always on the next gig or the next bottle. Now
he had to go through a goddamn UN interpreter to find
out how his daughter was doing. Hell, he'd been sober
for sixteen months. Are some things never forgiven?
"Your daughters really love the show?"

"Yeah. They say it's funny. And they think you're
cute. Especially all the Weight Watchers stuff and how
you can never lose any weight."

"Great."

"Rebekah's not happy with Martin." Lenny looked at
the edges of his fingers. Martin was the fella Donna was
seeing. He was extremely patronizing to Rebekah, al-

ways asking her how old she was and never inviting her along for quick trips to hardware store or Carl's Jr. for lunch. "I mean Carl's Jr. isn't filet mignon at the Waldorf. He could invite her along."

"Yeah. I get wanting to be alone at the hardware store, however—power tools are sexy."

Lenny laughed. "Come on. Let's go to the Blue Parrot. I'll buy you a ginger ale."

FIVE WEEKS INTO HIS COMEBACK, AFTER THE FOURTH episode—three episodes before the dating-Lionel's-teacher debacle—Dreyfuss was called to the Santa Cruz police station. His daughter had been arrested—fifth-degree misdemeanor for accompanying her friend Fawnee who stole makeup from Walgreens. Fawnee was charged with shoplifting.

"Fawnee, what kind of a name is that?" Dreyfuss hurried Rebekah along toward his Prius. The sky, a hard blue, glared off the roof. "And how could you just stand by and let her do it?"

"I didn't just 'stand by.'" She opened the car door and sighed. Fawnee never had much. Her mother had troubles holding down jobs. She raided her daughter's room, finding jewelry trinkets from various boyfriends, and hocked them at a local pawnshop.

"Look, I don't care about her problems. You have a record. Now you won't be able to get into Stanford—"

"I don't have a record. Fifth degree is nothing, the cop told me—"

"I don't want you hanging out with that girl. I don't want you shopping with her anymore. I don't—"

"Dad, you're not going to tell me what I can and can't do."

"She's dangerous. She's going to ruin your life—"

"She's not going to ruin my life—"

"Then why did you let her steal?"

"I told her not to. She did it anyway. Jeez, Dad. It's only cheap makeup and cheap makeup's expensive—"

"I don't want you seeing her. She's a barnacle, glomming on."

"God, you're such a snob. Just because she's low income, she's a *barnacle*."

"She's a thief, a regular goniff."

"Goddamn it, listen to you and all that goddamn entitlement. Dad, you're about as cool as the Beach Boys."

He clutched the steering wheel and pulled away from the police station. For the rest of the ride home, they didn't say much of anything. "I still have a soft spot for 'Surfin' Safari,'" Dreyfuss said.

DREYFUSS DIDN'T LIKE THE PAINTING ON THE WALL: a Confederate general seemingly shielding his eyes from the sun; nor was Dreyfuss crazy about the carpet—a red that looked pink that was trying to look red as if its very existence depended on being gender neutral because it just couldn't make up its mind which way to define itself.

LeGrand stood by the edge of his office desk. "I read your detailed memo of what's wrong with the show. Ten single-spaced pages. The *War and Peace* of television grievances. Sit down, Johnny—" He adjusted his bath robe and directed Dreyfuss to a red brocaded chair that looked kind of green.

The actor shrugged. He wanted out of his contract if things didn't change.

"We'll talk about that, but first, seconds ago I saw you squinting. You don't like the Civil War general?" He pointed behind him as if he were about to part the Red Sea.

"No. My eyes are just sore—"

"I got Excedrin Migraine, Advil, Claritin—"

"No, no. Who is he—the General?"

"How the fuck should I know?" LeGrand laughed. "Picked it up at a garage sale. Thought it added authority to the joint." He raised both eyebrows. They were poised to do a two-step. "Can I get you something? A Coke, ginger ale?"

"I'm fine." Dreyfuss looked at the ribbon lines, ridges along the lapels of LeGrand's robe.

"Sixteen months sober. That's nothing to sneeze at."

"Thanks."

He smiled again, and then his cell phone rang. "I'm not even from the South. I'm from Queens. My great-grandparents were immigrants. Jewish."

"Jewish?"

"Yeah, I know. Those same relatives changed the family surname from Granatstein to LeGrand. They picked a French name just to fuck with everyone." He slapped his thighs, picked up the phone, and apologized, saying we all know how anti-Semitic the French are. It was his seventeen-year-old daughter Melanie and they talked for several minutes about buying a new car (her idea) or getting a used one (his) and then something or other about love.

LeGrand rubbed his chin, smiled. "You think there's a difference between love and luv?"

"Huh?"

"L-o-v-e versus l-u-v?"

"Sure there is." One was more serious, the other playful. One suggested a deep commitment, the other a kind of sexual swagger, a fear of commitment.

"Wow." LeGrand tapped the glass top of the desk. It seemed Melanie's boyfriend always referred to her in his texts as "my luv," "l-u-v," whereas she wrote of him as "my love," "l-o-v-e."

Dreyfuss leaned forward, hands poised. This conversation, right here now, was the kind of stuff he wanted to see in the scripts. Real issues. Questions of love and identity, not lame retreads of old 1980s plots in which the only variable changed is that the Bomber is now forty-two instead of twelve.

"Hey, people love you. You're a fuck-up. The Bomber drops more bombs in his relationships than the allies did on Dresden, baby. That's your character: a little lost—"

"A little?"

"Okay, a lot."

"I want better stories—I want—"

"Okay, okay. The l-o-v-e versus l-u-v thing—I'm open to that. I'll memo that to the writers. Open-Door LeGrand that's me."

LeGrand laughed, so did Dreyfuss, albeit reluctantly. Even the general in the painting seemed to be laughing.

"I'm getting you loosened up. That's what I like to see. The old Johnny."

"Well, the old Johnny still thinks there are some

problems with the little old sitcom."

LeGrand's phone lit up. "I'm sorry, my daughter's always got drama going on." The conversation detoured into bees disappearing from the planet and digressed to commentary about honey and Winnie the Pooh's lack of masculinity.

He pressed the red icon. "I understand where you're coming from Johnny my boy, but the audience is eating this up. We just got signed on for thirteen more shows on USA."

Dreyfuss sighed.

"God, Melanie's such a Diva, but I love her." He apologized again for keeping the phone handy, but one of Melanie's friends from school might need to stay with the LeGrands for a while. Her boyfriend kicked her out and, well, Melanie helps everyone. "She's a regular *Flying Nun* of Santa Cruz. Flighty but with good intentions. Sally Field was so cute."

"Sally Field? Look—"

Just then Michael's cell phone rang for the third time. LeGrand kept the conversation short. "That's Melanie. Fawnee needs us."

"Fawnee?" *The* Fawnee, the goniff?

"Yeah, I know. Sounds like a character out of Bambi. That's the girl's name. The one in trouble. And since we don't have Thumper and all the creatures of Mr. Disney's mythical forest, we're going to go help. We'll talk about this identity-thing while helping." Helping involved offloading Fawnee's things from an apartment in Aptos and bringing her here to Michael's. The police would be on hand for protection, but Fawnee wanted more men around just in case her abusive boyfriend went all BP-oil. He shrugged the red robe off his shoulders. Underneath was a fresh-pressed polo shirt with a tiny alligator on it. "Come on, it's showtime."

"Boy, I didn't know that the Bomber was so fat."

Fawnee wore khaki pants and a bandanna that sported an Iron Cross insignia. Her ruddy, narrow face seemed to bleed into her washed-out brown hair, and her left eye wandered. Melanie, wearing faded jeans with her white-blonde hair tossed over her angular shoulders, shrugged and smiled sheepishly at Dreyfuss. "I mean, I knew you were fat," Fawnee said, "but I didn't know *that* fat. I guess TV makes you look thinner."

"I guess." *Usually they say it's the other way around.* TV images make you look ten to fifteen pounds heavier, but Dreyfuss didn't care to explain nor discuss his weight on the drive from Santa Cruz High to Fawnee's apartment. He had been self-conscious about the weight gain for some time and couldn't drop more than ten pounds. As he promised himself to bike more on weekends, Fawnee chuckled about how much she loved the show, especially those funny turns of phrase that the Christmas Goose said like *I depreciate that.* "That's funny."

"Oh, you mean the malaprops?"

She looked puzzled, her left eye trying to find him.

"You know like 'I depreciate that' instead of 'I appreciate that.' Or, 'let me regurgitate' instead of 'let me reiterate.'"

"That's what that is?"

"Yeah, he's using the wrong words."

"I didn't know the words were wrong. I just thought they sounded funny."

"Well, yeah."

Dreyfuss now called Rebekah on his iPhone. He wanted to tell her he loved her but couldn't find the words. "I just wanted to say—"

"I know what you wanted to say, you forgot my birthday. You always get it confused. I come the day before Kennedy's assassination. Not after."

"Right. The twenty-first, not the twenty-third." He had totally forgotten. "I'm sorry." And then he told her he was with Fawnee and helping her move out of some low-life's apartment.

"Dad—"

"Sorry. No censor."

"How did you get dragged into helping?"

"Long story. Look. I got a gift in the mail for you from Amazon," he lied. "Be looking for it."

"Sure Dad. Love you."

"Yeah."

He hung up, pulled up Amazon.com on his iPhone and glanced at the two girls in the car. "What do you get a girl who just turned seventeen?"

"Beats," Fawnee said.

"Yeah. Beats," Melanie agreed. "They're a way-cool set of headphones."

"Beats it is," Dreyfuss shrugged and clicked "place your order."

He then called Donna. She had texted him earlier that day about Cagney, wondering if he wanted him for the weekend. It was his turn for custody. "You know he looks like a gangster," she now said.

"He's a Chocolate Lab."

"Men."

"What?"

"You know I'm proud of you. How long's it been? Fifteen months."

"Almost seventeen."

"Wow. Martin's a shit."

"What?"

"*Men*. I already said that, didn't I?"

"You've been drinking?"

"Look when you come to get Cagney, you can stay for supper. We can talk. I want to talk. You want to talk? I'd like to talk."

"Sure."

"Men." The word suddenly had three syllables. "I have been drinking. Ironic, isn't it?"

INSIDE THE APTOS APARTMENT FAWNEE'S VOICE WAS full of combustible octane. "What the fuck? Where's my fucking shit, Tony? Huh?"

"It's right there, bitch. I packed it for you. It's ready." Tony leaned against the doorframe to what used to be their shared bedroom, his black T-shirt riding above his belt. Two of her bags were stuffed and standing upright ready to go. Another girl, with tattoos on her arms, including a spider-web on her left elbow, stood off in the next room alongside the TV. Positioned by the main doorway was a lanky cop, his Popeye arms folded with command presence. An older, freckle-faced cop stood by the kitchen, occasionally talking into the headset by his left ear. Dreyfuss nervously looked over at LeGrand who grinned absently. Melanie was helping Fawnee pack, gently whispering "dial it down."

"Dial what down? Where's my goddamn food stamps?"

Dreyfuss, too, wished that Fawnee would dial it down. Each of Fawnee's utterances ping-pinged like hard baseballs off aluminum bats.

"I got 'em," Tony said about the food stamps. They came to this address didn't they? He paid the rent, so they're his.

"That's bullshit," Fawnee snapped, and then literally shouted, "A Mr. Officer," and they all talked for a while. The older cop, a dead ringer for early '70s Martin Milner, told Tony to give Fawnee the stamps—she's the single mom, give her the stamps.

"But her kid's not even here," Tony said. "Her mom's taking care of the kid—"

"That doesn't matter. They're in her name, aren't they? Hand her the stamps."

"Cool. That's copasetic."

"What?" Fawnee's voice smacked a two-run double.

"You should read some books once in a while, Dumbass," Tony said.

"Fuck you, you fuck-face fucko."

A text message arrived from Donna. *Cagney's wandered off.* How*d it happen? *It doesn't matter.* It matters**how*d it happen?

Donna put the dog out, asking Rebekah to watch over him—Mom needed to nap—but neither tied the dog to a stake.

I'm sorry. Give us break. We've been searching for for-ty-five minutes. No luck.

After much haranguing from Fawnee and prod-ding from the two cops, Tony reluctantly surrendered the stamps, and then sulked from the room with arms raised as if he were about to have his rights read to him. He paused by the tattoo girl and kissed her cheek. Drey-fuss's gaze drifted onto the girl's arms. A tattoo on her left said "sweet," another on her right said "baby."

Minutes later, Dreyfuss and Melanie loaded Fawnee's gear.

Where could his dog be? Nobody wants an old dog—there's silver in his face; his eyes are rheumy; he breathes like a goddamn chain smoker. Did he wander the woods to die? "God, Fawnee's kind of difficult, isn't she?" Dreyfuss said to Melanie. LeGrand was gone. He had followed Fawnee into the building.

"She is." Melanie shrugged and held a hand up against the sharp sun.

"But you're a good friend."

"Yes, but she's a bit awkward." The fat comments were a little out of control. "She didn't mean anything by it. She just says things." Fawnee really likes the show, Mela-nie confirmed, and enjoys John as the Bomber. Together they watched last week's episode and Fawnee laughed and laughed. "She asked me to ask you for an autograph. She's kind of shy."

"She's shy? The queen of F bombs?"

"Yeah. Believe it or not."

"Okay." He'd give Fawnee an autograph, he promised. "I agree with you by the way on love, l-o-v-e versus luv, l-u-v. There's a big difference."

"Thank you." She leaned against the closed hatch of her father's Escalade and rubbed the top of a chipped fingernail. "So Daddy told you about that, huh?"

"Yeah." Dreyfuss looked at his shoes, layered with dust. "I hope—that—"

"Your daughter's a pretty cool person." She shielded the sun with her left hand. "Student council treasurer and all."

"Yeah." Dreyfuss smiled weakly. He didn't know about that. Rebekah had never told him. "She's always been responsible—taking care of money and books would be a natch."

"I don't know what to do—this whole l-u-v thing."

Donna texted again: *Be nice to Rebekah. She feels terrible.* "I'm sorry, I lost my dog—and—"

"Cagney?"

"Yeah." Dreyfuss too now leaned against the Escalade. The tips of his shoulders were hot with sun. "Talk to your boyfriend about l-o-v-e versus l-u-v." Should Dreyfuss have put the dog down six months ago? Just yesterday Cagney started wheezing while simply lying under the kitchen table. "Be up front, Melanie. What's the worst thing that can happen?"

"I find out he doesn't love me and feel rejected?"

"Well, yeah, that sucks, but isn't it better to know? He should know how you feel and you should know how he does." He paused. "I don't know."

"No, that makes sense."

Just then the lanky cop and his partner ambled to their cruiser. The lanky one was the driver—it was the opposite of *Adam-12*.

"They're leaving?" Melanie raised an eyebrow.

Dreyfuss hurried over to the cruiser.

Since they were here at Fawnee's request, the older cop explained, and she told them to leave, they were leaving.

Dreyfuss thought the situation too volatile. "Okay. I'll stick for a few minutes." The older cop's freckled face and easy-going eyes belonged in a Coppertone ad.

"Thanks."

"Hey, you play Johnny 'the Bomb' Lambertino. Love *Still the Bomber*." Last week's show was a hoot. Dating his son's teacher was a great touch. So real. "I got in trouble when I dated the dispatcher. She's also a temp teacher at the school." He laughed. "I think you should keep dating her. The kids can get over it. Mine did."

"Okay."

Fifteen minutes later, Fawnee, followed by Michael, trundled down the stairs of the apartment. A thin crinkle creased her lips.

THE RIDE BACK TO THE LEGRANDS WAS QUIET FOR THE first thirty seconds or so and then Fawnee gave one long monolog: Tony still loved her and Tony would always remember her. Their time together was special and she was a special girl and when she wanted back he was there and Velvet, that's the girl with the tattoos, is just a friend, they share a room but they're just friends, they're not sleeping with each other, they're just friends. "I know that, I know that's true. Tony told me." Sometimes they hug, Tony said, but that's just because they're lonely, and

Fawnee believed in those type of hugs because Tony said it was so, so it was, and whenever she wants back in he'd be waiting because what they had was special like a good story you can't forget, love notes in a bottle floating in an ocean and getting rediscovered, and theirs is a story that's memorable like those bottles, and he was keeping that special chain she got him to remember all the love they had. "He really misses me," Fawnee said. "He kept my chain. I still have his." She played with the dusky gold band cutting her neck with a thin line of dirt.

Was there ever such a moment as this strange tortuous car ride on the new and improved *Still the Bomber*? Was there ever a moment where a lie is recognized by all but the speaker and left to let stand so that the speaker can preserve his or her dignity? Isn't that what happens in life sometimes? We hide things from each other, keeping dark truths from escaping into the lies that float around us because we'd rather wait for the lie to run its course before allowing the diffusion of truth to filter into that hollowed-out space. To be wise is to know when to dispense knowledge and when not. When does one take the risk? This was not the time.

WHEN THEY ARRIVED AT THE LEGRANDS, REBEKAH was waiting at the edge of the front lawn, shoulders narrowed, reading her cell phone.

"I'm sorry about Cagney." She looked away, eyes floating marbles. "I didn't think he'd run. He never runs."

He reached to hug her and she turned, leaning in with her shoulders, gently fanning his back with a hand.

"It's okay."

"It's not okay. I screwed up."

"We all screw up—"

Fawnee was now crying. It was a dry cry and she didn't want comforting. Melanie and Michael and Rebekah and Dreyfuss carried her plastic tubs and suitcases and black velvet light posters and sand art bottles shaped like flamingos to the basement while Fawnee stood in the hot sun and smoked a cigarette. When they returned she was lighting a second one. Dreyfuss couldn't believe how fast she had inhaled the first.

He signed an autograph for her on the back of a brown envelope and wrote, "Get your shit together— John Dreyfuss." He thought of signing it "love" but that would be too much. He did leave her his phone number, however. If she needed anything she should call. And in a few days, he'd talk to the publicity department and send her an autographed photo.

Fawnee thanked him and said she was sorry about saying he was fat. He wasn't *that* fat. Just a little bit fat. "I just can't seem to talk to people." She looked through his left shoulder. When she gets nervous she either insults people or swears at them.

"I depreciate that."

She laughed again, tossed her cigarette, and headed into the basement.

Melanie thanked him too. Her jeans were birch bark white, like the color of sky.

"So, Big Guy, where do we go from here?" LeGrand's left eyebrow cocked with mischief.

Dreyfuss shrugged in the medium cool of early evening. "You know Lenny agrees with me? He thinks there should be changes to the scripts too. He just doesn't like to make waves—"

"Sure, sure." Hadn't he noticed, LeGrand pointed out, how Fawnee and Melanie liked the show?

"The cop too," Dreyfuss confessed.

"He likes it?"

"Yeah. And let's not forget Lenny's daughters. They think I'm, quote, *cute.* Close quote."

"You're a good actor, Dad," Rebekah said, her eyes slightly creased. Dreyfuss couldn't tell if they were colored with admiration, accusation, or a mix of both.

"What do you mean?"

"I don't know. You're so sincere when you're acting." She touched the bottom of an elbow and looked into the sun.

"Yeah."

"Thanks for helping Fawnee. And I'm so fucking sorry about Cagney. I love that dog." She leaned over and kissed her father's cheek, and he wondered if it was, in part, a shared moment of forgiveness.

Two months later, Cagney was still missing. Dreyfuss repeatedly phoned the humane shelters and animal control but nothing. As time drifted, Dreyfuss settled into the loss of his dog as a strange trembling comforted him. Initially, he felt cheated of closure, a final goodbye, but as day faded to day Dreyfuss realized Cagney had been saying goodbye to him all along: sleeping by his feet as Dreyfuss napped on the couch; nuzzling next to him as he watched afternoon ballgames; kissing him for handing over a Milk-Bone. The following month, at Dreyfuss and Katz's insistence, an offbeat episode of *Still the Bomber* aired. Critical response was mostly favorable. Some accused the show of having "jumped the shark"; "Nix on the Rabbling Social Crit," *USA Today* screamed in its 26-point headline; others, like movie critic Ray Carney, felt a deepening of sadness: *Still the Bomber* was now boldly exploring the "doubts that haunt us all. That knowing voice of dissatisfaction that so few have the courage to respond to." *TV Guide* echoed Carney's enthusiasm, calling it "one of the 100 greatest shows of the post-*Seinfeld* era. Heartfelt and existential. Must-see television." In this later-to-be-Peabody–nominated episode, the Bomb's fourth-grade son Lionel befriends a homeless man at the local bus station, bringing him extra sandwiches, cookies, and chunks of cheese. The man, an alleged Iraq war veteran and former undercover cop, tells tall tales of heroism and how an encounter with a highly sophisticated derivative of Agent Orange gave him debilitating hallucinations. Streetlights often blur into the comet-like glow of 4th of July sparklers. One afternoon, the man asks for an advance to purchase a nice suit for a job interview, and Lionel withdraws all the money he had saved from a summer of mowing lawns—close to a hundred dollars. Two days later, Lionel sees the man, half-asleep on a bus station bench, stumbling awake with drink, acting like he didn't know the kid, because deep down he's ashamed for not becoming the person the kid wanted him to become. He pushes Lionel away with words, saying the L-Train looks like a nuked-out version of Gilligan, as in *Island*, only Lionel's not as cute, just big-eared and goofy. That evening, Lionel burns all of his comic books and action figures in a huge backyard bonfire, saying he didn't believe in pretend anymore. The Bomb tries to soothe him, eloquently stating how art and imagination make life worth living, but his son believes only what's real matters; everything else is a lie. The Bomber, as inky colors burn and plastic melds into a glob of a lost planet, tries to explain the value of emotional truths, that all art, from the four-color pages of Steve Ditko to the films of Steven Spielberg, contains pockets of the real, the gritty subtext of each story, but Lionel, eyes closed, fighting tears, stays at the only level he's comfortable in. There is no pulling him back to the shoreline of art. He is adrift in acrid plastic and pages that burn, black ashes curling the sky.

According to Chelsea

❦

A CCORDING TO CHELSEA, IF JOHN CASSAVETES
were Swedish, he'd be regarded as one of America's greatest filmmakers. But critics like Pauline
Kael didn't get his work—they called him self-indulgent.
Self-indulgent? No one calls Ingmar Bergman self-indulgent, but if he were an American from New York
they would.

Chelsea always says uninhibited things like that and
I love it. We get together three or four times a week, usually early afternoons to talk movies or watch movies or
talk about the articles I'm writing. I'm a cultural critic, "Our Man in the Midwest," for *Beyond X*, a hip 'zine
out of Toronto. From Iowa, I write about pop culture
old and new and how it shapes our lives. I also wrote a
controversial piece on Jews becoming white. "Jack Black
is Jewish," the article begins, "but you wouldn't know it
from the white-bread roles he plays."

I liked that opening sentence, the play on *role* and
roll. Anyway, recently I also tackled *Snapped*, an Oxygen
Network fave about women behaving badly who lose it
and kill their partners. One chemist triggered a stun gun
to immobilize her ex, then tossed him alive into a fifty-five gallon drum full of hydrochloric acid. "Bitches," I

can hear sweat-stained men, in NASCAR caps, yelling at the TV, while sipping a cold one. "Shame on you," Chelsea said, as the afternoon sky turned a weird shade of green. She agreed that the secondary audience—angry men—may indeed be the main audience for that series, but I ought not to make assumptions about the viewers' backgrounds. "Come on, Wally. It's like you reached into a bowl of stereotypes and came up with a cliché." Her green eyes creased with the color of the sky.

"True. You've got me there." I held up my arms and promised to rewrite it.

She leaned against the couch in my apartment, sipped orange juice, and nodded. We've known each other for four months and she's always flipping me much-deserved shit.

Today she wore a charcoal-gray sweater and scarf. She always dresses nice.

And after we watched Bergman's *Through a Glass Darkly*, which she found wonderfully depressing, she wondered if I thought marriage didn't work.

I'm divorced. My wife, a college professor, left me for a young hot shot creative writer: Pushcart Prize winner, book with Penguin, another forthcoming, blah-blah-blah-blah-blah. Chelsea's divorced too. She's a part-time secretary in the math department—twenty hours a week, full benefits—and her husband, a math professor, left her for a student. Her most recent relationship with Tyler, director of Get Gone Graffiti, (a cleaning service), is up and down. I think this is one of the down periods.

"What do you mean, I mean, about marriage?"

"Well—" She turned and looked at me with this incredible energy in her eyes that kind of scares me because it's so blinding—it's like she takes you in completely. She said she disagreed with what I had to say about *Get Smart*, season 4. I had argued that Max's marriage to 99 dragged the show into domestic entanglements and took away from the comedy. Max was funnier when he was single. She said that she liked my article overall, how I contextualized things: the 1960s, the murders of RFK and MLK, and how a mood of uncertainty crept into the show as occasionally members of KAOS went unpunished, but one thing she was certain of was that marriage on the show worked and 99 was tops in her book.

"I like 99 too. Who doesn't like Barbara Feldon? But I just don't think marriage on the show worked."

"I disagree," she said, and then looked through my shoulder, because she could sense my shyness. "Is it just the idea of marriage on the show or marriage in general that you object to?"

"I don't know."

According to Chelsea, it was the latter. I think she might be right.

TYLER SHOWED UP AT MY DOOR A WEEK OR SO AFTER I first met Chelsea, saying he appreciated how I was helping her with the apartment, finding shit: a chintzy particle-board desk for the computer, a red lamp, and a philodendron for the damn cat to chew on. I took it the pet wasn't his.

Tyler wanted to pay me for the gas, but I said I did it as a neighbor. He insisted, his eyes hard-edged stones, a corrugated five-spot in his left hand. Getting rid of graffiti in Cedar Falls had become a sprawling business, he said. Scrawls of blocky letters were everywhere: behind the coffee shop, under the overpass, and along the red bricks of our local utilities company. The cleanup made it hard for him to chauffeur her around—he didn't know why a woman in her forties still insisted on driving a 1979 Pinto. "Damn thing's always breaking down." He shook his head and gnawed at his upper lip as if it were hardened chewing gum. Take the money. So, I did. Lincoln seemed unhappy.

Later, Chelsea thought it was weird that Tyler was so possessive. She pointed between me and her. "There's nothing here."

I like Chelsea. But I would never jeopardize anything by encroaching upon her relationship with Tyler. And I knew him, or of him. Waterloo West. The hair was thinner than I remembered, the body less wiry. He was a year ahead of me in high school, and in summers had a blacktop business, smoothing driveways in the suburbs. During his senior year, a white phosphorous of rumors filled Waterloo. Some customers alleged that Tyler was overcharging them—as much as three times for supplies. Despite the haze of scandal floating about, Tyler wound up valedictorian and specialized in biochemistry at college. I guess he came up with a chemical mix that attacks hip-hop words and symbols without beleaguering the buildings.

I once joked, flirted even, with Chelsea that is, that I loved talking to her and sometimes found myself so attracted to what she says, especially when she's quoting me and my work, that I have to look at her eyes, her hair, her face, in order to avoid looking any other places, "and I never ever read any T-shirts you're wearing."

"I don't wear T-shirts," she said.

"I know," I said. "I'm just trying to make light of things. I'm a minimizer."

"Why do you minimize all the time? You shouldn't do that."

Why, indeed. Maybe she likes me too. I don't know. Sometimes I feel like I'm still in seventh grade. I'm forty-three; she's forty, and I fear that I do "like her like her."

THE FIRST THING ABOUT CHELSEA THAT SCARED ME was how much she knew. She said that I had sad, sorrowful eyes, the kind that carried pain and fatigue and hurt. I was surprised by her insight because I thought she was the one who had been hurt and that's why I had left my door open.

The night she moved into the apartment across from mine didn't go well. Tyler's voice was on edge—he was frustrated and his words were buried under shuddering boxes, knocked about end tables, and bookcases hitting baseboards. I think he even threw some things. Glass popped like underwater firecrackers.

Anyway, her voice, through the walls, was a flash of an earring—brittle yet bright. By contrast, Tyler's words were heavy and dank like the inside of a cave. He yelled at her again, and then a door violently closed.

The next morning I left my door open while washing dishes and she knocked, asking if I had any eggs, and I offered her some and said I had heard her crying. "I wasn't meaning to pry. Well that's not exactly true. I was standing by the door, your door, with a very large glass."

That made her laugh, and then she sat down and offered to show me a tattoo—*Vidi*, "That's Latin for I saw." She didn't care for the other part of the quote because she didn't like Julius Caesar. "Fascist creep." But she liked the idea of seeing things, and then told me she had another tattoo, on her left breast—that one I wasn't going to see—and then she made that comment about my eyes. And before I knew it, I was telling her all about Ginger, my ex, and how she left me for a creative writer, someone with more ambition.

I smiled and as I talked about Ginger I wanted to tell Chelsea what I had really heard outside her door. Tyler felt that her love for him was always compromised, not fully there, and it hurt like hell. I wondered if he hurt her in return. Faint bruises shaped like Georgian Bay and Lake Huron marked Chelsea's biceps. She noticed that I noticed and said it was nothing. Passion. "Some men scream your name. Tyler squeezes." She forced a laugh. "I guess it's his kind of personal tattoo."

"I guess."

Shit, when she was a kid Chelsea liked weaving her fingers through the metal webbing of her parent's living room fan. As the twist of blades cut the heat she wondered how close she could come without nicking her hands. She held them up. "I still have my fingers."

WEEKS LATER, CHELSEA SAID THAT I WROTE beautifully and she couldn't believe that Ginger would leave me for a writer because I'm a writer. And the topics I covered were "very ambitious."

200

"Fiction is more sexy," I said. I guess I'm just John Cassavetes to her new boyfriend's Ingmar Bergman.

"Bullshit," she said, her lower lip all pouty before a smile creased her eyes. "You're both. Cassavetes and Bergman. But that's beside the point. Divorce, separation, these things often come down to," she paused, "tension."

"By tension, you mean sex?"

"Yeah. It's always there among men and women."

"No."

"Sure. Why do you think so many straight women love hanging out with gay men? I'll tell you why—tension isn't hovering, that's why."

There was a long pause, maybe too long as I wondered about Tyler—how much tension did he create when she didn't want to have sex? The other night I think he was shattering plates in the sink. "I'm not gay," I said.

We were sipping tomato soup at my kitchen table.

"I know." She shrugged and adjusted the long braided scarf around her neck. My apartment was always a little cold. "I'm sure if I wore T-shirts, you would know what every one of them said."

"Maybe so."

"You haven't given up on love have you?" Because you shouldn't, she said, reaching across the table and lightly tapping a finger against the back of my hand. Her frizzy hair was frosted and her eyes the darkest green. She told me that I was a great listener, but the sadness of my eyes had to do with a celibate retreat from experience.

"Celibate?" I tried to deflect her insights with a

"whatever," but she saw through the mask.

"How did she hurt you?"

"My ex?" I shrugged and wiped at a crescent-shaped spot on the table. "I really don't want to talk—"

"You know what I do when I'm hurt? I get a tattoo."

She had three. Each scarred into her skin as comfort for a sad turning point. A dolphin on the ankle for the time she was turned down by New York's Academy of Dramatic Arts; *Vidi* on the inside of her left wrist after a turbulent relationship with a high-school teacher ended—she was sixteen, his student; and on her left breast a Gaelic symbol for fertility. That was an act of humility. After spending a semester in Ireland she realized she would never create anything as beautiful as the prose of James Joyce.

Needles make me nervous, I told her.

Then she confessed to thinking about getting a fourth tattoo. A hammer and sickle for Tyler. "You know he wants me to straighten my hair? He doesn't like how frizzy it is. And he wishes I dressed nicer. I dress nice. I'm a secretary."

I nodded, and then talked some more about Ginger. For the past two years we had drifted apart: she into her world of academe and Carson McCullers scholarship, me into my cultural criticism. In the evenings we hardly spoke to each other and often she was going out with fellow faculty at UNI, networking, without inviting me. "And then she started reading this guy's stuff—I saw the manuscripts lying around—instead of reading my work—and—why does love have to be fleeting? Why can't it last?"

"I don't know." Things with Tyler weren't so good, either. Everything she does is wrong. He wants time apart but still wants a relationship, only separate apartments. She bit the edge of a finger. "He also said I was too loud. I'm too loud when I sing along to the car radio; I'm too loud when I buy groceries; I'm too loud on the phone. Am I too loud?"

"Yeah, you are, but I find it endearing."

"Thanks."

I liked talking to Chelsea. In my past relationships I've always been a kind of Dean Martin conversationalist. "You ever notice how he sings? The shallow part of his chest? Light. Not serious?"

"Why would anyone not want to be serious?" she said.

"Do you really think Chaplin is narcissistic?"

I nodded and said, yeah, I do. We were walking away from the marquee lights of the Art Theatre. We go there once a week and had just screened *City Lights*. "I mean, that ending, come on. The closeup, the flower, that smile. It screams, love me, love me please." Chaplin was totally oblivious to his audience—it was all about himself and his need for approval.

Outside trees sparkled with a shimmer of snow, a light foggy haze, and the street was quiet—one or two cars. Chelsea wore a camel coat and a beret. She looked marvelous.

"What's wrong with love?"

"Nothing. Love's great, I guess," I said. Across the street from us, in the snow-beaded window of a coffee shop, I thought I glimpsed Tyler sipping from a dark mug. His hair was heavily moussed, and he wore a sweater, the cuffs rolled past the elbows. His hand made lopsided circles, like a child's, against the store's frosted glass.

"You guess?"

"Yeah. But with Chaplin, his desire to be loved is all encompassing; it's too self-absorbed. I prefer Keaton. He's clever, inventive, and less—"

"Touchy-feely?"

"Well, yeah."

ACCORDING TO CHELSEA, I'M UNCOMFORTABLE WITH intimacy. Real conversations. I often have to make jokes to lighten the mood. "You're right, I'm always protecting myself," I said one afternoon while we were watching *Cabaret*.

"Are you scared of me?"

"A little. Now stop asking such deep questions—I want to enjoy this pretentious film."

"I don't think it's pretentious."

Of course she wouldn't—it was her choice. The second part of the double bill was my choice, a depressingly gritty masterpiece, *The Friends of Eddie Coyle*. We were on a '72-'73 kick.

"Well, don't be scared." Her goal was to match me up with someone. She said there was a secretary in Philosophy and Religion, Nina, who was single. I said I wasn't ready for any of that.

"Why not?"

"I'm not ready. Let's watch this drivel—it's so bad, it's good." Minnelli was singing.

It was hard to match Chelsea's energy, but through movies and TV shows I could talk to her comfortably.

On one of our first afternoons together, eating cold pizza and watching Howard Hawks's *Bringing Up Baby*, I told her all about the cozy confines of the Art The-atre: the clanking seats that needed to be reupholstered, the lingering mildew smell of the aisles, reminiscent of wet woolen sweaters, and the people, characters, ec-centrics in fedoras and bright lipstick huddled in the dark. You see, one night, I said, these two women in pea coats, bracelets on their wrists the size of anchors, and a puff of perfume, arrived late at the Art and asked me to move over so that they could sit together. "Of course you didn't, because you're anal retentive," Chelsea said.

"No, well, I am, but that's beside the point." I get to the theatre forty-five minutes early so I can have my ide-al seat: row thirteen, seat ten, nine seats to my left and right. It's the ideal vantage point to watch a film. "I'm not giving that up. I tried to explain this to the girls us-ing geometric logic and advanced calculus, but they just nodded and then sat next to me, on either side of me. And all through the show, a revival of Sidney Lumet's *Prince of the City*, I became so aware of their breaths and breasts that I couldn't concentrate on the film."

"That's too bad," Chelsea had said, laughing.

"Thanks. Your sympathy is overwhelming. Why can't my life be like a Hollywood movie? One with a happy ending"

"You know Tyler wants me to see a therapist?"

I didn't know what to say.

"A week ago, Tyler said he thought our love should

be a series of collisions, car wrecks, and I guess we aren't colliding enough or something—"

I thought about the clink-clink-clink of a fan and fingers. "Who does he want you to see, Josef Mengele?"

"That's not funny."

"I'm sorry."

We were quiet for a long while but I wouldn't apologize further—I didn't like Tyler. To me, he was a darkened sun. The logo for his business was three granite G's in a hard, uncompromising font like him.

Fuck it, Chelsea said. "Finish the story. Tell me about the girls in the pea coats."

So I did. If my life were like a Hollywood movie, the girls would have been hanging out in the lobby after the show and I would have approached them, or them me, and struck up a conversation about the film—no, no, they wouldn't want to talk about *Prince of the City* yet. Too soon. They needed to let the ideas of the film resonate. "Stillness has to set in," one of them would say. So, we'd talk about the film from last week, Aronofsky's *The Wrestler*, love and loneliness, and how the ending was all wrong. Ram shouldn't die coming off the final turnbuckle. Instead, here's how I would end the film, if it were a Wally Bober production: the Ram should retire, go back home to the trailer court, and the final shot of the film would be a tableaux: the Ram standing on his front porch holding two trash bags, looking in the direction of Tomei and her pickup truck parked out front. Tomei is pensive, looking in his direction, the driver side door open, but unable to move toward him. Fade to black.

"That's beautiful," she said. "You can still approach Nina."

"No. Look at me—I'm a neurotic nut. No."

"You are a nut."

"Thanks."

And then she kissed me on the cheek. "But lovable."

Following the story of the pea-coated girls, Chelsea asked me to take her to the Art, and we've been going ever since. Usually Wednesdays. Church night. Tyler cleans business buildings then.

Now, taking short, quick choppy steps to keep up with me, Chelsea smiled and read the Art Theatre's program, *In Focus*. "Hey, look, next week the Art's showing *All Through the Night*."

We had watched the Bogart film the week before at the apartment and she wanted to see it on the big screen. She loved that film because it was such a weird mix of genres: comedy, gangster, romance, and wartime melodrama.

"It's like my moods—never consistent."

I laughed.

"Tyler doesn't want me to see you anymore."

A sharp nudge pinched my shoulders and suddenly my stomach was full of glass. "It's up to you what you do," I said.

"He's watching us from the coffee shop."

I didn't turn to look. "I thought he had the local community center to do tonight."

"Maybe there was too much snow."

And without knowing why exactly, I reached for Chelsea's hand, squeezed it quickly and let go.

"Bogart and the cheesecake scene? With the Sgt. Bilko guy? That's funny." She just can't see anyone eating cheesecake with gloves. "I love cheesecake. But with gloves on?"

"Bogart's not wearing gloves—while he eats—?"

"You sure? I swear—"

"Anyway, I can't eat cheesecake anymore," I said. "I have to watch my sugar."

Poignant. According to Chelsea that's one of my favorite words and I guess it is. I end a lot of articles with it. A zippy, one word sentence: "poignant," as if I'm resonating pithy truths for my readers, but the move in my essays has become stock, formulaic. *Poignant.* Corny is more like it.

Anyway, earlier in the day I had been stuck on an article on model Betty Furness and her 1950s TV spots for Westinghouse's Studio One anthology series. I did have some insights on a sexy woman in high heels and bright dresses belying a masculine, scientific discourse: Betty tells us, with great efficiency, that the fifteen vents on the Westinghouse iron make it more effective for dampening fabric; the removal of blades from the center of the Westinghouse washer and accompanying tilted basket get all of our clothes clean without wearing down the fabric. But beyond the initial paradox of the feminine sales rep and the masculine science behind her words I had nothing new to offer. Nothing about this was poignant or ever would be. Perhaps it wasn't an article after all.

Serendipity, however, is a weird thing. Here I was

struggling with images of 1950s femininity and the construction of rational order through engineering technologies when who should come to the door but Tyler demanding that I return the china plates. Said china plates were loaned to me last week by Chelsea when I entertained some friends from the newspaper—where I also freelance—and we ate French cuisine—crepes—and watched three of Jean-Luc Godard's 1960s films including *Vivre Sa Vie*. Apparently the plates belonged to Tyler—his mother bought them as a housewarming gift—and he wanted them back.

"Plates? What does a guy want with plates," I said, somewhat incredulously, as I sipped orange juice by the kitchen sink.

"Look, Wally, I just want them—" He gnawed at his upper lip, a left hand on his hip. He was a lot bigger than he was twenty-five years ago. The sweater he wore crinkled his chest, his jeans were torn in the left knee, and his moussed hair was perpetually wet: a controlled look, exuding a faux-relaxed ease. Even Tyler's five o'clock shadow looked like it belonged in a catalogue for men's clothing.

I stacked the eight or nine plates from the cupboard and handed them to him. He said he thought that Chelsea was spending too much time with me. Everything was fine until I showed up with the car rides, and the talk, and the holding hands.

"That was just—"

"Affection?"

"Yeah, that's all." The words were dry, brittle crumbs. Chips of glass returned to my stomach. For a second I felt that he was going to hit me with the plates, and then I just didn't care.

I didn't care that one time in high school he bloodied a kid in the gym lockers for stealing his lunch money; I didn't care that he was tired of me, tired of Chelsea's talk about the wonderful articles I was writing, like the one on Obama and 1968 and the intensity of actors like Clarence Williams III of *Mod Squad* and Otis Young of *The Outcasts*. "Yeah. That's one of my better ones actually. Those two actors brought dignity and a smoldering presence to the small screen. Where are these African-American role models today?"

In my irrational randomness, words were not quite fitting the moment; my internal censor was on vacation. Hovering on the brink of a whupping, lake-sized bruises were already forming under my eyes. Tyler shifted the plates to his left forearm.

"I'll tell you where those people are," I said. They aren't on TV. TV's for the rich. The new art's happening on buildings. Hip-hop. Graffiti. Don't you ever think about what you're erasing, Tyler?

"What? Art? Come on. It's just empty gang symbols—"

"Gang symbols? It's somebody's voice, it's a response to the systemic racism of our culture."

"'Systemic' what? Wally—they don't own the buildings—"

"I'm not talking about buildings!" He never did get it. In high school, his tastes ran from the middle of the road to the crude. Favorite actor: Sylvester Stallone. Best book: *The Power of Myth* by Joseph Campbell. Band:

Guns N' Roses. Idea of fun: inviting the football team over for a night of poker, cigars, and VHS porno. Business practices: buy supplies cheap, charge for services high. Damn it, Tyler, you're messing with a people's means of expression, silencing their presence. Goddamn Philistine.

I guess I was saying all that Philistine shit out loud, because the next thing I knew my nose was pop-popping like a roll of Black Cat firecrackers and my shirt gushed red. I didn't know blood could be that bright.

A COUPLE OF NIGHTS AGO, CHELSEA SAID THAT THE swelling around my left eye had gone down and she was pretty sure my nose was broken. "That son of a bitch, Tyler." I absently shrugged and she softly kissed the hurt spots and wondered why I had never asked about her name. What's to wonder? I said.

"Okay—" Her single mom was really into soccer and during junior year studied abroad in England and took in a Chelsea/Liverpool match and decided to name a future daughter after the city and its blue-clothed football club.

"No shit?"

"No shit."

"I got a niece, Rebecca, who's crazy about English soccer. Hopefully she won't decide to name a daughter Liverpool."

Chelsea laughed.

"Actually, I'm joking. She likes Chelsea."

"The team or me?"

"The team. She's never met you."

"Why is that?"

"Why? I don't know. We're not a couple. I hardly ever see my brother Manny as it is—"

She wondered if I could drive her to Wal-Mart. The Pinto was in the shop: master cylinder, water pump, something, and she needed to get a few things for her apartment: plants, a tea cozy, and some plates.

LAST NIGHT CHELSEA WAS STANDING AT MY DOOR, holding up two trash bags.

"What's this?"

"Guess."

"Uh, you need help with your trash? What?"

"No. Remember *The Wrestler*?"

"Aronofsky's film?"

"The girls who sat on either side of you?"

Oh, yeah. The twins in their pea coats and my re-written ending with a pickup truck. "You're Mickey Rourke?"

"Yeah." She held the bags higher.

"I'm not Marisa Tomei," I said emphatically.

She refused to lower the bags and laughed. For weeks we had been talking about popular culture and she felt for half that time she had been really talking about us, about love, without saying it, but now she felt I needed a visual clue, because I was kind of dense on the love front, and this was her way of saying my life could be a Hollywood romance. "What do you think *this* has been about?"

"What?"

"This. Us."

"Us? Uh, friends getting together to talk and watch films and—"

"I wouldn't be here just to watch films. I spend a lot of time here—"

"You like me?"

"I told you the tension was hovering. I was tense around you—I mean, in a good way. Weren't you tense around me?"

"Please lower the bags. Look, if I were to get a tattoo, it would be of a soccer ball. Right here." I pointed over my heart.

"Don't say that." She thought it was sweet but also distant because she knew I'd never get a tattoo, what with my whole needles thing. So, according to Chelsea, I was Dean Martinizing it, minimizing again.

"I'm sorry."

"I left Tyler. For good this time." She wasn't interested in seeing a damn therapist—there was nothing to mend. Even though he didn't break the china plates everything else was broken.

"Wow." I didn't know what else to say so I resorted to Brando-esque incredulity. Remember the scene with Rod Steiger in the car—*On the Waterfront*? Steiger pulls a gun on Brando, threatens his brother, and Brando utters a soft, wistful, "Wow." Why can't I be authentic and let real feeling come through? Instead, I resort to modes of being, actions and mannerisms from film and TV. Maybe I should write a book: *All I ever Learned I Learned at the Movies*. It would be a depressing book.

Her eyes watered. She no longer loved Tyler, the passionate aggression, the white bursts of violence. So she gave back the china plates and the power tools. "Actually the power tools were mine, but I didn't want to argue about it."

According to Chelsea, I guess, I am Marisa Tomei, the stable one. Oh, well. I reached for her trash bags, plunked them by the kitchen, and directed her to the living room sofa. She cried into my shoulder and I held her and we sat there for a while, and for the first time I noticed her perfume: bright and fresh like the frost of fog on tree limbs outside. I told her I hadn't been honest. "I do like you. Like really like you."

"So we are in seventh grade."

That made me laugh. And then I had one of those moments, like in a John Cassavetes movie where the lead characters let their masks fall, stop pretending, drop the role playing, and become authentic people through an epiphany. *Shadows* ends with three of them. Anyway, I held her hands and told her about Ginger, really told her, how not only had we drifted apart but I had fallen out of love with her—the last two years of our marriage we were just absent friends, nodding at each other, now and then, and I just wanted to be able to feel again, without worrying about falling out of love, because that's the worst feeling in the world, that fleetingness, that inability to find constancy, and I never want to experience that again.

"But isn't it better to try to love again, to—"
"Maybe."
"I wasn't being honest either. I love you—"
"Really?"
"Yeah."

"I guess the moviegoer gets the girl after all, huh?"

"I guess."

"I think I love you too, but I'm still not going to get that tattoo to prove it."

She punched me in the shoulder. "Will you stop with the minimizing?"

"Okay. Okay."

And then she suggested that we do something totally different tonight. Instead of going to the movies, let's drive to New York City. No popular culture. No TV, no radio, no nothing. Just us.

"New York?"

"I'm packed." The two trash bags were full of her clothes. She wanted to take to the open road, maybe find an art deco nightclub in the big city and eat cheesecake.

"I can't eat cheesecake," I said.

"Live a little," she said.

About the Author

Grant Tracey is an English professor at the University of Northern Iowa, where he teaches film and creative writing, and has been the fiction editor of the *North American Review* for over fifteen years. He has published nearly fifty short stories, three collections of fiction, and articles on Samuel Fuller and James Cagney. His collections are *Lovers & Strangers, Parallel Lines and the Hockey Universe*, and *Playing Mac: A Novella in Two Acts, and Other Scenes*. Twice nominated for a Pushcart Prize, Grant was the recipient of an Iowa Regents Award for Faculty Excellence in 2013. In addition to his writing, editing and teaching, Grant has acted in over twenty community theater productions. He is currently working on a crime novel set in 1965 Toronto.

Photo by Mitchell D. Strauss

A Note on the Text

The book is set in Adobe Minion Pro. Minion is a digital typeface designed by Robert Slimbach for Adobe Systems in 1990, and Minion Pro was added to the family of typefaces in 2000. Minion was inspired by Renaissance-era type.

CPSIA information can be obtained
at www.ICGtesting.com
Printed in the USA
FFOW03n1350100416
23077FF